His
DEAL

REBEL ROSE

Copyright © 2018 by Rebel Rose

All rights reserved.

This is a work of fiction. Names, characters, places, brands, media and incidents are either the product of the author's imagination or are used fictitiously. The author acknowledges the trademarked status and trademark owners of various products referenced in this work of fiction, which have been used without permission. The publication/use of these trademarks is not authorized, associated with, or sponsored by the trademark owners.

ISBN-13: 978-1-948113-09-0

ISBN-10: 1-948113-09-0

CreateSpace Independent Publishing Platform

ISBN-13: 978-1-982049-31-7

Formatting by Indie Formatting Services

Cover Design by Indie Formatting Services

NOTE FROM REBEL ROSE

This book contains BDSM situations involving dubious consent and physical restraint. These situations can be triggers for some readers and erotic for others. If you view BDSM as abuse then this book is not for you.

If you should choose to continue, enjoy.

1

EMMA LIA GRANT

MON BEBELLE?

I may not know a lot of Cajun French, but I know what mon bebelle means. My doll. Such an unexpected choice of nickname for the submissive he plans to dominate... and hurt.

Kitten. Pet. Minx. Those seem like more typical submissive monikers. Not something as endearing as mon bebelle. But what do I know? Maybe he's used all of those classic names on his other submissives and is running out of the usual subjugating ones.

"Would you like to have breakfast on the veranda?"

Tristan would like to have breakfast instead of his first go at dominant sex with his new submissive? That's unexpected.

He laughs, and I realize that my expression has probably given away my thoughts. "Sorry. I'm just surprised. I thought you'd want to go to my bedroom and crack open the kinky cabinet as soon as I said yes."

He chuckles louder. "*The kinky cabinet?* That's what you've named it?"

I nod, a smile breaking through my exterior. "Yeah. That's what it is."

The chifforobe is beautiful. It looks like a piece you'd have seen in the house when it was built in 1857... but open the doors and drawers and you'll get a not-so-nineteenth-century surprise.

"The kinky cabinet. Fitting name. I like it. And as much as I'd love to crack it—and you—open, you drained my tank last night and this morning. I need protein and time to recharge my batteries; I want to be at the top of my game for our first scene."

Translation: he wants his balls to be full when he dominates me for the first time. I noticed that he has a thing about that—filling me with his cum. No man has ever done that inside me. It hasn't been possible with my trio of defenses against pregnancy: the pill, condoms, and pulling out just in case.

Not a single one of my boyfriends has ever convinced me to deviate from my anti-pregnancy routine. But Tristan did. And I caved so easily.

The act of a man coming inside a woman—it's not something that I've ever given much thought. I've always considered the guy's orgasm to be the finish line, but it doesn't end there for Tristan. He gets his rocks off even more on coming inside me and then watching it drip out of my body. It's bizarre and hot at the same time.

"How do you feel about frittatas for breakfast?"

I'll try anything that Ray cooks. "Sounds good."

"We'll sit on the veranda and talk while we wait."

It's only nine o'clock, and I can tell that the sun is going to be merciless today. My hair is already sticking to the back of my neck. And the steaming-hot black coffee that Tristan brought to me isn't the least bit refreshing.

"I hate black coffee."

He lowers the cup from his lips. "I am a man who remembers details, and I distinctly recall your telling me that you take your coffee black, just as I do."

I guess there's no reason to not tell him the whole truth now. "I did, but it was a lie. The coffee they brought to us in the hotel suite was scalding hot. I was going to throw it in your face and escape if I got the opportunity."

"Well, fuuuck." He looks like he's letting that one sink in for a moment. "You're not still planning to maim me when I least expect it, are you?"

I probably shouldn't tell him that I was also planning to stab him in the eye with an ink pen. Or choke him with the lamp cord. Or slice him open with shards from the mirror after I broke it. "Not anymore."

He touches the healing scratches on his face. "You did an excellent number on my face. These lacerations are going to take a while to heal."

"I'm sorry I did that to you."

"I'm not angry about it. I liked the way you fought me." He smiles and a single dimple appears in his right cheek. "I think I'd look pretty badass with a scar across my face."

"I hate to break it to you, but you're never going to look like Mufasa. Those scratches aren't deep enough to leave a scar. Plus, your face is far too pretty to be scarred."

He scowls. "Let's get one thing straight: I am not *pretty*."

He can deny it all he likes. He is very pretty but in a masculine Matt Bomer or Rob Lowe or Henry Cavill kind of way. "Okay. Handsome is a more suitable description."

He takes a sip of his hot coffee and looks at me over the top of the cup, smiling. "Scale of one to ten, what am I?"

His face, his body... he's perfection. Completely off the charts, but I'm not telling him that. "Mmm... maybe a seven."

"I'm *maybe* a seven?" A chuckle rumbles in his chest. "Would you like to know where you fall on my scale?"

I shrug, my very intentional attempt at appearing indifferent to his opinion of my looks. "Sure."

"I can't put a number on you. You're infinity. The most beautiful woman I've ever seen."

I'm pretty. I'd label myself a 6.5. Maybe a seven when my hair and makeup are on point, but the most beautiful woman in the world? That's the second time that he's told me that.

And I call bullshit.

"You are aware that because of our deal, I'm a sure thing?" He has me right where he wants me. Bastard. "You don't have to woo me."

"I'm a Dom. I don't *woo* my submissive. When I tell you that you're the most beautiful woman that I've seen, it's because I mean it." I hear annoyance in his tone.

I'm preparing to dispute his statement and tell him that I think he's full of shit when Ray comes out of the house, interrupting our debate. He places a plate in front of each of us, and the argument I had for Tristan is instantly forgotten when I see and smell the food.

"Two spinach-and-mushroom frittatas. Will there be anything else, sir? More coffee?" Ray asks.

"Miss Grant would like some juice. She doesn't care for coffee."

"Would you like apple or orange?"

"Orange would be great. Thanks."

We eat without conversing for a while before Tristan breaks the silence. "Are you enjoying *The Thorn Birds*?"

"I am, but I was surprised by the eighteen-year age gap between the hero and heroine. And I didn't expect the story to begin while she was a child." I went into it expecting a love story between two grown adults.

"Their age gap isn't a whole lot more than ours."

Fourteen years. Tristan had almost lived a whole other life

by the time I was born. "I don't feel like you're fourteen years older than me."

"Is that because you feel older or because you see me as younger?"

"Maybe a little of both." I unsuccessfully try to stop my smile from spreading. "Unless we're talking about sexual experience; you definitely don't seem younger when it comes to that."

"I hope you aren't saying that I don't compare to the young bucks you've been with?"

"There is no comparison."

He stops eating and stares at me. "I need you to clarify that."

Does he think that I could possibly be implying that the twenty-somethings I've been with are better than him? That's amusing. I also find it a bit entertaining that he's baiting me to hear my praise and approval.

He may be this dark, demanding Dom, but he's still such a man-child.

"You're the best that I've ever had." And he knows that.

"You haven't seen anything yet, Miss Grant." A mischievous grin spreads. "But you're going to. Very soon."

When? The word is on the tip of my tongue, but I don't say it aloud. I'm afraid to hear the answer.

Change the subject, Emma Lia, or you're going to work yourself into a tizzy.

His hair is damp, and he's wearing jeans and a T-shirt, not his usual business-suit attire. "You aren't going to work today?"

"No. Someone kept me awake all night; all she wanted to do was fuck. I'm exhausted."

A light huff expels from my lungs. "Pfft... I think you

mean that you kept her awake all night because all you wanted to do was fuck."

He chuckles. "I didn't keep her awake. I know because she snored for two hours before I left her bed this morning."

My mouth opens and I gasp sharply. "I... do... not... snore."

"You do snore."

"You stayed and listened to that for two hours?" Who would put up with listening to that annoying sound for two hours? I know I wouldn't.

"I like watching you sleep."

He watched me sleep? I can't decide if that's sweet or creepy. I'm leaning a little more toward creepy.

"You must like hearing me snore as well since you listened to me for two hours." Which is just embarrassing.

"It's cute when you do it."

"I don't care who you are. Nothing about snoring is cute." I know because my nana sounds like a lumberjack.

Change the subject, Emma Lia, before he tells you that you also sleep farted. "I was planning to go by my apartment today. I need to pick up a few personal things if I'm going to be staying here."

"*Since* you're going to be staying. Not *if*."

I will need to choose my words more wisely around this man. He's testy about some things. "Okay. I need to pick up some personal things *since* I'm staying."

"Have I not provided you with everything that you need down to your hygiene products?"

I feel like saying, hell yes, all the way down to my tampons. But I keep my mouth shut on that issue. "You have, but I'd like to get my laptop and iPad. And I have some cash that I'd like to move to a safety-deposit box." I would die if someone broke into my condo and took that twenty grand in my closet; I worked hard for that money.

"Wait until another day to do it. I'm playing hooky from work to stay home and have alone time with you."

It's difficult to have alone time when there are two other people in the house. "Is it really alone time if Ray and Claudia are here?"

"Would you like me to send them away for the day?"

I don't know what Tristan's going to do to me. I may scream. I may cry. I may say to hell with all of this and flee. I don't want anyone here to witness whatever happens. Plus, I just think that sex, vanilla or otherwise, should be private.

"I'd be more comfortable if I knew that other people weren't listening to us."

"Consider them gone."

He places his fork on the plate and tosses his napkin on the table. "Are you finished eating?"

It's delicious, but my stomach is in knots. "I am."

He sits back in the chair and looks at me. "Go to your bedroom and take off your clothes. Everything. Kneel next to the bed, facing the door. Sit on your lower legs and feet. Bow your head and keep your eyes lowered. Do not lift your face when I enter the room. I'll tell you when you may look at me."

My brain absorbs his words, and I try to picture the described position in my head.

"Do you understand?"

"Yes."

"Yes *what?*"

Dammit. That's going to take some getting used to. "Yes, Sir."

"I will come to you as soon as I finish making arrange-ments with Ray and Claudia, and we will begin your first lesson. And don't forget that you are to address me as Master inside of the bedroom."

My head becomes swimmy, and the warmth leaves my cheeks. It feels like ants are crawling beneath the skin covering my hands.

He gets up and stands behind me, placing his hands on my shoulders and squeezes with gentle pressure. His grip releases and squeezes again. The kneading feels good to my tense muscles.

Leaning down, his mouth hovers over my ear. "Close your eyes and breathe, bebelle. Slow and deep. Place all of your concentration on moving air in and out of your lungs."

In and out, slow and deep. I do as he instructs, and my head feels normal again after several nice deep breaths. I feel more like me.

"Better?"

I didn't say a word about the way I was feeling on the inside. "How'd you know?"

"I'm already becoming in tune with your body. But it's only the beginning. I'll eventually know everything about it just as you'll know everything about mine."

Knowing each other's bodies on that kind of level is highly intimate. It's something that should be shared between affectionate lovers, not near strangers like Tristan and me. And certainly not as part of a deal to keep him from sending me to jail.

Blackmailing bastard.

I go to my bedroom, and I don't mess around once I'm there; I won't have long until Tristan arrives, and he's going to be in full-on Dom mode. I know because I saw the raw, untamed desire in his eyes. I heard the deep, unwavering command in his voice. It frightened me. But it also excited me.

I breathe deeply and lower myself to my knees. I sit on my

lower legs and feet and place my palms on top of my thighs just as Tristan instructed. I bow my head and look at the floor, studying the design of the wool rug to take my mind off of what's about to happen.

Doesn't help. I'm trembling like a lamb about to face a lion.

I'm motionless, listening for his footsteps. Th-thump. Th-thump. Th-thump. My heart is beating so damn hard in my ears that it drowns out anything else. Feels like I'm in the middle of one of those dreams where I'm being chased by a monster, but I can't move. I can't run. I can't scream.

Tristan leaves me in this position for a while, much longer than expected. I wonder if this is a test to see how long I will stay in this position without moving or if I have Claudia to thank for the delay. She's probably giving him shit about leaving because she doesn't want this to happen.

The wood floor creaks to my left, each sound from the wood planks coming closer. He instructed me to face the door. I assumed that he meant the hallway door and not the one separating our bedrooms so he's thrown me for a loop. And I'm not in a position—literally or figuratively—where I need to be thrown for any more loops.

"Fuck. I've dreamed about you being on your knees for me since the first time I saw you in my casino, but the fantasy is no rival for the reality." His fingers touch the bottom of my chin and he lifts. "Look at me."

I lift my face, and I see two things as I move my eyes up his body: one, he's already naked. And two, his cock is huge and hard.

His eyelids are weighted with lust, and a partial smile is tugging his mouth to the side. That single dimple has shown up for the show. "You have no idea how fucking gorgeous you are on your knees looking up at me right now."

He steps closer and pushes his fingers into the back of my hair, his hand forming a tight grip at my nape. "Suck me."

I've given head before but being told to do so in such a demanding manner is a new one for me—though not at all unexpected coming from him.

I grip the base of his cock, and he watches it disappear into my mouth. The tip glides over the surface of my tongue on the way in, and his salty pre-cum coats my taste buds. I like the way he tastes.

"Ohhh... your warm, wet mouth feels good."

I use my tongue to follow the bulging vein on the underside of his cock, and his fingers tighten around my nape, pulling me closer. "Take it in all of the way," he whispers.

I close my eyes and suck him in until the tip of his cock hits the back of my throat, instantly making me gag. I try to not think about it, but a reflex is called a reflex for a reason.

I pull away when the unsexiest sound in the world comes out of my mouth a second time. Fucking humiliating. "I'm sorry."

"Don't be. I love that sound. It turns me the fuck on because it means you're obeying and taking my cock deep." His hand pulls my head toward his dick. "Do it again. And don't stop because you gag."

I take him into my mouth again, and Tristan uses his grip on my hair to control the pace and depth of my mouth sliding over his cock. I unsuccessfully fight the urge to gag and warm tears trickle down my face until they drop from my chin to the floor.

This man is literally fucking my mouth.

He sucks air in through his teeth. "This is better than I dared to hope for, bebelle."

Bebelle. I hear him call me doll, and I instantly want to please him.

And I have no idea why.

I suck harder and cup his balls with my hand, alternating a light squeeze-and-release motion, rolling the firm spheres between my fingers.

"Oh, fuck that feels good."

Everything between my navel and knees involuntarily tightens and twitches and tingles when he praises my oral skills. I squeeze my thighs together when I feel the slickness growing between my legs, and the realization hits me: sucking his dick is turning me on. And the more he likes it, the more I enjoy doing it.

"Fuck, I don't want you to stop, but I'm going to come before I want to if I keep letting you do that."

He releases the back of my head and pulls his dick out of my mouth. Copious amounts of saliva drip from my mouth and chin as well as his dick. But it's unnecessary. I can already tell that my pussy is wet for him.

"On the bed. Hands and knees."

I wipe my mouth and chin as I rise from the floor. I move toward the bed, but he grasps my wrists, pulling me so we're face-to-face. His hands move up, cradling the sides of my face, and he kisses the wetness on my cheeks from my eyes. "I love tears when they're the right kind."

"These are the right kind?"

"Yes."

He releases me, and I crawl on all fours onto the bed. "You've pleased me, bebelle, but I still need to spank you for trying to leave me."

I liked the spanking he gave me a few days ago. I won't mind another one.

I place my open palms on the mattress and slide them forward, lowering my head and leaving my ass in the air. "I'm ready to count for you, Master."

A loud groan rumbles from his chest. "Perfect answer."

The mattress dips when Tristan climbs onto the bed behind me. "You liked it when I spanked you, didn't you?"

"Yes, Master."

"I liked it too. A lot. And I'm going to like it this time too." His palm flattens on my butt cheek, and he rubs it in a circular motion before digging his fingertips into my flesh. "Your safe word is rouge."

"Rouge?" Odd choice.

"It means red, and that's the color your ass is going to be when I finish spanking you." Shit. "Don't say the safe word unless you can't take more. Understood?"

"Yes, Master."

"Are you ready?"

"Yes, Master."

I try to convince my muscles to relax, especially my glutes, but the fuckers won't obey. They have a mind of their own, and they don't appreciate my trying to fool them into thinking that nothing is about to happen.

I jolt when Tristan's hand comes down hard on my left cheek. And the intensity gets away with me; it's so much more painful than the first swat he gave me over the dining room table. "One, Master."

My body is most definitely not relaxed when the second swat comes. Fuck, it stings my skin. "Two, Master."

I press my face into the bed and bite the comforter, preparing for the third. And I jerk hard when Tristan's palm lands on my ass. "Uhhh."

"Count, bebelle, or we start over."

"Three, Master."

Oh my God. How many of these am I getting? He didn't tell me.

Four. Five. Six. Seven.

Rouge. Rouge. Rouge. I bite the comforter to keep the word from rolling off of my tongue.

Ten. I bet that I'm getting ten.

Hot tears sting my eyes and mucus rushes to my nose. Shit, I don't think that I can take three more painful swats like these.

But what if I'm wrong and he intends on giving me more than ten? What if his favorite number is twelve? Or fifteen? Or what if there isn't a magic number. What if he keeps doing this until I collapse?

I don't know what he wants from me.

My sharp inhalation is unintended, as is the sob that follows, and I press my face into the comforter harder. I concentrate on inhaling and exhaling slowly while he finishes this.

I squeeze my eyes shut and imagine myself anyplace except here. But it doesn't help when the next swat lands on my cheek.

Eight. Nine.

Ten. It has to be ten. I don't have it in me to take more.

"Ten, Master." A loud sob escapes my lungs.

"That was the last one, bebelle."

My body collapses on the bed, my trembling extremities giving out beneath me. I'm out of breath. My muscles are jelly. The whole thing couldn't have lasted more than a few minutes, but it feels like I've just finished running a long marathon that went on for hours. I don't have the strength to do anything but lie beneath him like a lush.

He climbs over me, his front pressed to my back, and kisses the nape of my neck. Chills erupt over my entire body. "Do you think that I'm finished with you?"

I know better than to think that. I saw the extent of Tristan's sexual stamina last night. The man can go and go and go.

"No, Master."

"Good. Because I'm not."

Even though my ass is on fire, a surge of happiness blazes through me. I want his mouth on me again. I want more of that gifted tongue licking my pussy, and if I have to endure a hard spanking to get it, I'll choose that trade-off every time. It's that good.

His strong hands wrap around my wrists, stretching them outward, and he places my hands on the edge of the mattress. "Hold on to the edge and don't let go."

Don't worry. I'll have no choice when that magnificent orgasm hits.

He uses his knee to push my thighs apart, and his hips settle between my parted thighs, his erection nudging against my vulnerable entrance as he moves up and down as though teasing me. And not in a good way.

"What are you doing?"

"Shush, bebelle. You'll like it. I promise."

I twist and look at him with a mixture of fear and anger, abandoning my new role of submissive. "I told you no anal."

"And there'll be no anal... *today*."

There will be none tomorrow or the next day or the next or any day after that.

His hand moves between my legs and strokes my lips, igniting tingles in my core. "Mmm... who does this tight little pussy belong to?"

I step back into my role. "You, Master."

"Say it."

"My tight little pussy belongs to you, Master."

"Yes, it does. You're mine to play with. I can do anything I want to you. Do you understand?"

"Yes, Master."

Two fingers slip inside me. "Your pussy is so wet. Is that because you're a dirty little girl who wants to be fucked?"

His mouth is filthy. I can't believe that he had the nerve to call my language crass.

"Yes, Master."

He takes his fingers out of me and uses the lubrication on his fingers to make my folds slick. Preparing me. He's not going to be tame like he was last night—I'm seeing that in the way he's talking to me.

And I'm not wrong. He enters me with one powerful thrust, plunging so deep into me that his hard cock hits a bundle of sensitive nerves that can only be located somewhere near my womb. The sudden intrusion is unexpected and sharp. It feels as if he's trying to split me in half, which prompts a quick gasp from my mouth.

The animal-like growl I hear behind me is unnerving, and yet my body responds to it, growing wetter and stretching to accommodate his huge cock as it enters me from behind.

He fucks me brutally. No mercy. And I admit that I scream. Some are elicited by pain, some by pleasure, and the two intertwine until I can't distinguish between them.

His body lowers and he lies on top of my back, but not with all of his weight. The brunt of it is on one forearm against the mattress while his free arm comes around my body, his hand wrapping around my throat. His fingers press against the vulnerable vein at the side of my neck, holding my life in his hands. And I feel completely controlled by his iron grip.

He presses his mouth against my ear, and the pressure on the side of my neck increases. "I'm going to come inside you, and your pussy is going to take every drop. Do you understand?"

"Yes, Master." My voice is a strangled whisper.

He pounds into me harder, and the friction of the big head of his cock sliding in and out beneath my pelvic arch increases, hitting a sensitive area in the roof of my pussy perfectly. I can't recall any man ever doing anything to me that feels this way.

My breath, constricted, comes faster and shallower. The pleasure I feel is climbing at a rapid pace, and I have this incredible desire for more. "Fuck me harder."

"Don't command me," he growls. "And don't you dare come until I say that you can."

"What do you mean don't come?" I can't stop an orgasm from happening if he continues doing what he's doing.

"Fight it, bebelle."

Fight it? Is he kidding me? I've never been able to achieve an orgasm with intercourse, and now that I'm going to he wants to take that away from me. No fucking way. I want this orgasm.

His hand grips my throat tighter. "I'm your Dom, and I decide if and when you get to come."

I tense my pelvic muscles, but that only manages to make it feel better, bringing me closer to orgasm. "I can't stop it from happening. I don't know how to control it."

He slows his thrusts. "Ride the edge. Don't give in to it."

My entire focus is on the friction I'm feeling inside my pussy and not letting those uterine contractions begin; once the first one begins, it'll be over. I'll be at the point of no return. And he'll be displeased with me.

I'm relieved when the heavy feeling inside my core lessens, taking with it the urgency to explode. But it hasn't gone away entirely. "Please let me come. I'm so close."

"No. Don't let it happen until you have my permission."

His merciless thrusts return, and so does the climbing pleasure. "It's building again. I can't stop it."

"Almost there, bebelle. Hold on a little longer."

I grip the edge of the mattress and breathe deeply. It's the only thing that I have total control over right now.

The pressure on the side of my neck increases when he presses his fingers harder and I feel lightheaded, as though I might black out. "Come for me, bebelle. Now."

He pushes into me as far as he can and groans. "I'm coming so hard inside your tight little pussy."

The contractions in my pelvis tense and relax around his cock at least a dozen times before dwindling away. It's over too quickly.

He's lying on top of my back, his weight holding down my body. I can't move, but I don't think that I could even if he weren't on top of me.

He stays inside me until his softening cock slips out. Once we're no longer joined, he rolls to his back to lie beside me. "Be at ease, bebelle."

"Be at ease?"

"It means that you can speak freely. You don't have to formally address me as Master unless I tell you to resume your submissive role." He rises and leans over my body to kiss my shoulder. "I don't usually let my submissive orgasm, but I found out last night that your pussy is heaven when you come around my cock. I couldn't resist; there's nothing in the world like it."

"I didn't control the orgasm. I just got lucky with the timing." I might as well tell the truth.

"Thank you for being honest about that." His hand rubs my back, and it easily glides over my skin thanks to the sweat he deposited there when he was pressed on top of me. "There's an art to learning how to edge. I'll teach you how we can control it together."

"To edge?" Edge is a verb?

"That's when you build your sexual excitement to the point that you almost come, and then you stop and let it smolder. You deny yourself of an orgasm. After you build and deny several times, your body will explode when you finally do come. The orgasm is incredibly powerful, but it's time-consuming and takes a ton of patience. And self-restraint. I didn't have any of those things in me after I saw you on your knees in the submissive position."

He moves down my body, kissing along my spine, and slides his hand between my legs. "We have nowhere to be. Turn over and spread your legs. We'll begin your first lesson in edging."

He wants to teach me how to control my orgasm. Postpone it until it becomes explosive.

I'm okay with that.

Maybe this submissive thing won't be so bad after all.

2

TRISTAN BROUSSARD

Her cunt was so tight and slick. My cock was in heaven when I glided in and out of her. She was drenched because of me, because of the desire between us.

Mon bebelle enjoyed our first Dom-sub experience. Maybe as much as I enjoyed it.

Addressing me as Master came with pure ease for her; she was turned on by my dominance. She liked handing over all control to me. And I'm in no way surprised.

Submission can be learned, but for some it happens naturally. Those are the special ones. And mon bebelle is very special. She is my natural submissive. My counterpart. I'm even more sure of that now than I was the first time I saw her.

She is the one.

Mine.

My little submissive wanted my cum. Her greedy pussy clenched and relaxed around my cock over and over, milking every drop from my balls until I had no more to give.

She told me to fuck her harder. A command. It was gratifying but displeasing at the same time. Definitely worthy of another five swats across her ass, but I resisted the urge. Two spankings in such a short time span would probably overwhelm her. And I choose to overwhelm her in a much different way.

I've played with her pussy all morning. Rubbed her. Fingered her. Licked her. I've brought her to the edge of orgasm many times and then kept her climax at bay. Training her. "Should I let you come this time?"

"Yesss. Pleeease."

She squeezes her eyes shut when my fingers press harder on the walnut-shaped bundle of nerves inside her pussy. Her breath moves in and out through pursed lips. Desperate to come. All of the signs are there, but she's fighting it to please me.

"Look at me, bebelle. Eyes on me."

Eye contact. It's not something that I've demanded from my other submissives. In fact, I didn't want to look at their faces during sex at all, but Emma Lia isn't one of my trained subs. Everything about this relationship is going to be different.

She opens her lids, and our eyes connect. Her parted lips and tense facial muscles are a clear indication of the struggle she's experiencing.

"Come for me, bebelle." I move my fingers faster and the wet friction sound grows louder. "I want to feel your pussy quiver."

Her hand comes up and her fingers push into the back of my hair. She pulls my head to hers, and our foreheads are pressed together. Her grip is ironclad. It wouldn't be an easy escape if I tried to get away.

Her pursed lips open and form an O. "Oh... ohhh... ahhh."

I cover my mouth with hers, devouring her screams, and her entire body is trembling. She nips my bottom lip, and I immediately taste copper. Any other Dom would be furious and probably flog her ass until it welted, but I don't mind her bite. I'm sort of sick that way.

Her body begins to relax as the orgasm spirals down from its peak. She releases my mouth, and her breathing slows. My pride swells because I know what kind of breakthrough I've just made with her.

She's still holding the back of my head, and we're simply looking at each other. No expression. No words. Just eyes on eyes. And there's something truly penetrating about the way she's looking at me.

I remove my fingers and bring them to my mouth, sucking them clean while she watches.

She smiles, breaking our staring contest, and her body becomes toneless when her limbs fall to the bed. "I have never experienced anything like that in my life."

"You liked it?"

"One word can't describe that. It was agonizing... and astonishing... and amaaazing."

"I wasn't exaggerating when I said that edging takes a lot of work and patience when it's done well."

"It was done very well. My body is exhausted. I need a nap."

I look at the clock beside Emma Lia's bed. "Take a nap if you like. I'll wake you in a couple of hours, and we'll go out for a late lunch."

"You didn't sleep last night. I know that you must be tired. Stay and nap with me."

I'm exhausted. Staying in bed with her is tempting as fuck, but this is day one of our Dom-sub relationship. I don't want to send mixed messages to Emma Lia and cause confusion right off the bat.

"Don't have time to nap. I have calls to make since I'm not going in to work today."

"I made you come."

"You certainly did."

"I'm owed a key pull."

As if she needs to remind me. "You are. Would you like to get up and do it now or after you've napped?"

"Hmm… I'm so tired. I don't think that I can get up and do it right now."

I'm elated that she isn't jumping out of bed and racing to the box. I'm even more hopeful that I'll be able to keep her long enough to mold her into what I want, and then she'll choose to stay of her own accord.

I lightly smack the fleshy part of her hip. "Rest, bebelle. I'll come back in a couple of hours."

I allowed Emma Lia to sleep longer than two hours. I could say that I got caught up with calls for work and time got away from me, but that would be a lie. I went into her room a little after noon with the intention of waking her, but I couldn't do it when I noticed how angelic she looked.

Dark hair splayed on the pillow beneath her head. Ivory skin against the white sheets. One of her rosy nipples peeking out from beneath the sheet covering her body. I just wanted to enjoy looking at her sleeping figure for a little while… just in case she happened to be the luckiest person in the world and pulled the right key on her first try.

One minute of standing over her turned into an hour of my sitting in the chair in the corner of the room watching her. And I've postponed her pulling a key for long enough.

I place my hand against her upper arm and glide it up and down her silky, smooth skin. "Bebelle."

She stirs lightly, her baby blues peeking through narrow slits. And then those slightly parted lips widen, turning up on the outer edges, and a pair of dimples make an appearance. I can't remember ever being the one to bring that kind of smile to a woman's face. "Hey, you."

Hey, you. I've also never had a submissive that would say anything so casual, even when I allowed her to be at ease. The conversations I've shared with them have been stiff and formal. But I find that I don't mind the relaxed nature I have with Emma Lia outside of a scene, even when we're in the bedroom.

"Do you feel rested?"

"I do." She twists and stretches to see the clock. "And I should. It's a quarter after one. Why didn't you wake me already?"

"I hated to; you were sleeping so soundly."

"Does sleeping soundly mean that I was snoring again?"

"Just a little heavy breathing."

"Mmm-hmm."

She pulls the sheet up to cover her exposed nipple when she notices my staring. "I need to shower if we're going out."

"You've already showered."

"True, but I smell like sex now."

"I happen to like the way you smell after I've fucked you." The mixture of our body fluids is a divine scent.

"You like it when I smell funky?"

"You don't smell funky. You smell well fucked, and I like it. I also take pleasure in knowing that you're walking around with my cum still inside you. No shower."

"You're awfully bossy for a man who might not even be my Dom anymore after I pull that key."

Now that just pisses me off. "I *am* your Dom."

She shakes her head. "Not if I pull that key... which you owe me right now."

I don't allow people to hang shit over my head or to taunt me with anything, and I'm damn sure not going to let her.

I grab the sheet and yank it from her body. She's still naked, and I would consider taking advantage of that again if she hadn't just pissed me off so badly. "Get your ass up. Now."

She looks at me with wide eyes and then rises to a sitting position, sliding to the edge of the bed. "Give me a second to grab my robe."

I grip her wrist and lead her toward the door. "No robe, sweetheart. We're getting this shit done and out of the way right now."

She jerks her wrist free of my hold and stops in the hall-way. "You owe me that key. Why are you acting like an asshole about it?"

"I'm not acting. I *am* an asshole."

She follows me to my office and watches as I unlock the cabinet. I remove the box of keys and slam it on my desk. "Rules. You can feel of the keys for as long as you like, but you can't look at them. Once you pull a key, it won't go back into the draw box. Understood?"

"Understood."

She reaches into the box and moves her fingers around, digging for longer than I like. Makes me get worked up when I see the concentration on her face; this woman is a cheat with magic fingers. I worry that she's outsmarted me and come up with some kind of tactic for finding the right key. And that it will work.

Fuck, I realize in this moment just how unprepared I am to let this girl go.

What the hell is going on with the increased beat of my heart? And in the pit of my queasy stomach? And my damp palms?

She pulls a key and holds it up between us. "This is it. My freedom."

"Only one way to find out." I hold out the padlock. "Do you want the honors?"

"Sure do." She smiles and takes the padlock from my hand.

The key's shaft slides into the hole without a problem, and my heart jumps into my throat. Fuck, has she done it? Pulled the right key on her first try? It's not possible.

Except it is. She has a one percent chance of getting it on the first try. One percent isn't much, but it is a chance.

Her brow lifts. "Ready?"

"Go for it; I'm not worried." Lie. I am mildly panicked.

"Okay. Here goes."

She turns the key and nothing happens... with the exception of the smile disappearing from her face.

Thank fuck.

"Damn it," she hisses.

It's a dodged bullet. Another victory over this woman by fate's hand. It has decided that she is mine for a while longer.

I hold out my hand, and she places the key on my palm. "I'm still your Dom. I've only begun to show you what that means."

"What are you going to do?"

My eyes scan her naked body, and at least a dozen ideas come to mind. All of which will make her scream.

"Anything I want to do to you, bebelle." I let her think about that for a moment before I finish. "But later. Right now, I want to take you out."

She did a fine job of taunting me about the key, about

earning her freedom, about leaving me. It doesn't sit well. My little submissive must learn that I'm not one to be goaded.

I think Miss Grant needs to be introduced to the flogger soon.

3

EMMA LIA GRANT

"WOULD YOU CARE FOR SOME FRESHLY SQUEEZED lemonade, miss?"

I stop reading and place my book over my stomach, looking up at Ray through my dark sunglasses. "Does it have lots of vodka in it?"

"No, miss." Ray chuckles. "I'm sure it would be tasty with some Grey Goose, but Mr. Broussard would be unhappy to come home and find you sloshed."

"No. I don't think he'd like that at all." I certainly don't want to provoke Mr. Broussard again. Not after the spanking he gave me last night for teasing him about the key and my leaving. My ass has just now stopped stinging. But that orgasm after the spanking... it was worth it. And I had earned another key by the time he was finished with me.

Two keys down. That's two keys out of the way of pulling the right one.

"I would love some lemonade. Thank you, Ray." It's another scorcher today. I haven't checked the temperature, but it's an easy ninety.

Most people would be inside where it's cool, but I love

sitting in the garden behind the house. I find it peaceful. And the hot weather is fitting for my reading of *The Thorn Birds*. Makes me feel more drawn into the setting of the miserably hot Australian outback.

"Hey! Whore!"

Whore?

I stop reading and look in the direction of the female voice carrying from the back door. The former sub. Boy, has her attitude toward me changed since our last encounter.

"Hi, Claudia. How are you today?" She looks like hell.

"Fuck the niceties. I want to know what the hell you're doing to Tristan."

What *I'm* doing to him? The man is a Dom. You don't do anything to him unless he commands it. "Is that a serious question?"

"I'm dead serious, whore. I want to know what you're doing to him."

"First of all, stop calling me whore. I'm not here by choice. And secondly, have you met Tristan Broussard the Dom? I don't do anything to him that he doesn't tell me to do."

She crosses her arms and shakes her head. "I don't believe that for a second."

"I honestly couldn't care less what you believe."

"Tristan is different with you. Softer. How are you making him be that way?"

She seems to know an awful lot about my relationship with Tristan. "How do you know that he's different with me?"

She looks away, her eyes on the ground. "He told me that you kissed and that you *made love*."

I don't understand what Claudia wants from me. A confirmation? A denial?

She loves Tristan... and he's fucking me. Why is she putting herself through the torment of asking me questions about us? There's only one answer that I can think of: she is a true masochist who not only enjoys physical pain, but also emotional pain.

"I was Tristan's sub for more than a year, and he never kissed me. We never made love. He couldn't even fuck me face-to-face. I want to know how you made him do those things with you."

I doubt it matters what I say. She isn't going to accept that my relationship with him is different from hers. "I'm not his puppeteer. I didn't make Tristan do anything. He wanted to kiss me. He wanted to make love to me face-to-face. He's the one who wanted vanilla."

Vanilla. Her face jerks upward to look at me when I say that word. "Tristan doesn't do vanilla."

"Tristan does do vanilla. And he does it very well." I've never had better.

"He does it very well? What does that mean?"

"What do you think it means?"

"He made you come?" I hear the disbelief in her voice.

"So many times, I've lost count."

"You're lying; Tristan does not allow his submissive to come."

I shrug and pick up my book from my lap to return to reading. I'm tired of this conversation, and frankly, what we did or didn't do is none of her business. "Makes no difference to me if you believe me or not."

"Don't think for one second that Tristan will ever love you."

I look up from my book. "I don't give a fuck if Tristan Broussard ever loves me or not. I just want him to keep his end of our deal and give me what he promised." So I can get the fuck out of here and go back to my life.

"What did he promise you?"

"That's between us."

"You're going to fall in love with him. He's going to crush your heart, and when he does, I'll be there laughing my ass off."

If I were a weak woman like Claudia, that might happen. But I know who I am and what I want. And it's not Tristan Broussard. "He's a selfish asshole. I could never fall in love with a man like him."

"Let's revisit this conversation in six months and see what you have to say then."

Not gonna happen. "I don't plan on being here in six months."

"Good. Because I don't plan on your being here in six months either. And just so you know, I am going to win him back."

I'm about to tell her to fuck off when Ray comes out of the house, a phone other than mine in his hand. "Mr. Broussard has been trying to reach you, miss."

Shit. I forgot my phone inside. He won't be happy that I've missed his calls.

I take the phone from Ray. "I have a call to take, Claudia. I'd appreciate some privacy."

"Don't mind me."

Tristan is going to chew my ass out. That's not really something that I want Claudia to hear.

"Hello."

"Where have you been?"

Shit. He's mad. He'll probably use this as a reason to spank my ass again. "Just outside. I'm in the garden reading."

"You should have taken your phone with you."

"You're right. I should have. I'm sorry." I already know that an apology isn't going to save my ass if he wants to punish me.

"When I come home, I want you to be showered with your hair in a knot on top of your head. You know the way I mean. And your make-up... do it heavy with deep red lips."

Deep red to match my butt cheeks? "What would you like me to wear?"

"Nothing. I want you to be naked when I come to your room."

"Yes, Sir."

"Did I hear you say something to Claudia before you answered the phone?"

"Yes, Sir. Unfortunately."

"Is she harassing you?"

"Painfully so."

He mutters something under his breath that I can't quite make out. "Tell me that you want me to eat your pussy when I get home. And make sure she hears."

I look around to make sure Ray isn't in sight. "I want you to eat my pussy when you get home."

"Mmm," he groans. "Now tell me that you're going to come all over my face."

I would almost rather die than say these things in front of anyone. Even Claudia. "I'm going to come all over your face."

"Fuck you." Claudia's voice spews like venom through her clenched teeth.

I suspect for a moment that's she's going to attack me, but instead she spins around and stalks toward the house. A part of me is amused by her response after the way she just spoke to me, but another part of me feels sorry for her. She loves a man who will never love her back. A man who may not even be capable of loving a woman. A man who would be cruel enough to have me say hurtful things about what we're going to do in bed together.

"She's gone."

"What did she say to you?"

"It began with her demanding to know how I was making you change."

"And?"

I'm a little embarrassed to say the rest. "She told me that I was going to fall in love with you, and you'd crush my heart and blah, blah, blah. Just ridiculous shit like that."

"No woman should ever fall in love with me."

I laugh. "I don't need to be convinced of that."

"I'm glad you understand. I wish she had."

"What time are you coming home?"

"I should be there around six."

"I'll be ready."

"On your knees."

"Yes, Tristan. On my knees."

4

TRISTAN BROUSSARD

Three. Two. One.

My thighs are burning and quivering when I bend my knees and lower the weights to a resting position on the seated leg press. The fuckers don't need exercise after the workout they've been getting with Emma Lia since she accepted the terms of my deal.

I'm between reps when Easton appears by my side. "Sorry I'm late. I hope you didn't get your panties in too much of a twist while you were waiting on me. I know how you are about that shit."

Easton knows me well. "You lucked out this time, man. I was too busy thinking about my new submissive to notice that you were late."

He lifts his foot from the floor and stretches his calf. "Where in the hell did you come up with that one?"

"The Biloxi casino. Blackjack table. She's a professional gambler." I don't want Easton to know about our deal or that I'm blackmailing her into being my submissive, so I leave off the part about catching her cheating.

"How old is that girl? Or rather how young is she?"

"Twenty-two."

"Fuck, I haven't had a twenty-two-year-old in a long time."

Easton demands excellence. With the exception of Claudia, he isn't one to bother with amateurs and newbies. And learning takes time. You don't find many twenty-two-year-old experienced submissives walking around the club.

"What is her name again?" he asks.

Mine. That's her name. "Emma Lia."

"*Emma Lia*. Fuuuck, she's hot." He smiles when he says her name, and I want to throat punch him. I'm so fucking obsessed with her that I despise even hearing her name on his lips. And I hate that she is the reason behind his smile.

"She doesn't know anything about being a submissive, but I'm completely obsessed with her. I don't know how to explain it." The degree to which I want her isn't reasonable.

"I admit that I had a difficult time fucking Claudia when there was a hotter woman in the room. I actually imagined that I was with your girl instead of Claudia the whole time."

A bubble of fury inflates inside me. "You better be fucking with me."

"I'm not, man. I couldn't help myself."

"I am not cool with that." I don't want any man thinking about Emma Lia. Especially Easton. And especially like that.

"Whoa, fucker. Why are you getting so pissed off?"

I turn away to adjust the weight on the leg press, avoiding his question.

"When do I get my turn with her?" he asks.

I grunt and blow air through my lips as I straighten my legs. "You don't."

"I've always shared with you."

I slowly bend my knees. "And I've always shared with you, but this one... this one is different."

"I'm well aware of how different she is. That's why I want my turn with her."

His turn with her? No. Fucking. Way. "I've already told you, E. I'm training her to become what I want for my needs. Only mine."

He moves to the leg press beside me. "I can help you train this girl. Hell, think about how great she'd be if she had two Doms teaching her."

The thought of Easton touching Emma Lia makes me want to throw him through the fucking wall. "She's vanilla. I have to take things slow with her. Two Doms would freak her out for sure." Not that I would even consider letting him come near her.

"What have you done with her so far?"

"Beginner stuff—fucking, oral, edging, spanking. Basic submission and obedience." I choose to leave off the vanilla part.

"How was she?"

"This girl… she's a natural, and she can't be described. She's something that must be experienced."

"Which is exactly what I want."

I shake my head. "Forget about it, E. I'm not budging on this one." Not even for my best friend.

"You can be one selfish fucker sometimes."

Won't argue with that. "I've barely introduced Emma Lia to the lifestyle, and she's already fully embracing it. She pleases me in ways that I can't explain." Hell, her existence alone pleases me. "And she has the tightest pussy that's ever been wrapped around my cock. It's fucking amazing."

"Don't tell me that shit, man. Just makes me want to fuck her even more."

"Well, you can forget it." The girl is mine.

5

EMMA LIA GRANT

"Ray has outdone himself again. This French toast is amazing."

Tristan grins behind his coffee cup as I stuff another bite into my mouth. "What? Why are you smiling?"

His chuckle is deep and throaty. "You enjoy food."

"I enjoy *good* food. There's a difference."

"My subs don't usually eat much. They watch their weight."

I don't know what his other subs look like, but Claudia is on the anorexic-looking side in my opinion. "You like skinny girls." Statement. Not question.

I am not skinny, but he seems to like me just fine.

"I thought that I did."

I thought that I did. What the hell is that supposed to mean? "You need to clarify what you're trying to say."

"You have curves. I love the way they look, both in and out of clothes, and I love the way they feel when I glide my hands over your body. Gives me something to hold onto. That's all I'm saying."

"You like my hips and booty, don't you?" I have a great ass, and I don't even have to work for it. It's the one thing that I can thank my mom for.

"I fucking love your booty. And I'd love it even more if you'd hurry up and let me get in that thang."

It always comes back to that with him. "Sorry, Broussard. No can do."

"I'm going to get my cock in it sooner or later, bebelle. You'll see."

"No can do, muchacho, especially not after seeing what your friend did to Claudia."

Lines form on Tristan's forehead, and he shakes his head. "I really wish that he hadn't done that in front of you."

"I really wish that he hadn't either. I can't get it out of my head."

Tristan quickly looks at me. "You can't get Easton out of your head?"

"That's not what I said."

"Do you think he's hot?"

Wow. Tristan sounds like a jealous high school boyfriend. I shrug. "I don't know. I haven't thought about it."

"Well, think about it. Do you think that Easton is hot?"

The guy was good-looking, and his body was ripped. I would definitely take a second look at him if I saw him out in public. Unless Tristan was there—he'd definitely be the one that I couldn't take my eyes off of. "Yeah, your friend is hot."

"Do you want to fuck him?"

What the hell kind of question is that? "God, no."

"He wants to fuck you."

Am I imagining that Tristan sounds angry about that? "Your friend told you that?"

Tristan nods. "We worked out together this morning, and he asked me to share you with him."

Is that how the lifestyle is? You just go around sharing sex partners? "I hope you told him that you'd never share me with him."

A smile spreads on Tristan's face. "I told him no."

"Good. Because that shit ain't happening with me." *One Dom is more than plenty for me.*

"You don't have to worry. I will never share you with another. You're mine, bebelle. Only mine."

I am his... but only until I pull that key. And then I'm out of here.

"Will you be home at the usual time?"

"Planning to be unless something unexpected happens. Why?"

"I was thinking that I'd go to my condo today and then go by to see my family and Avery. Unless you need me to be here."

"I think today would be fine."

I don't have my car. I guess it's still sitting in the parking garage at the casino in Biloxi. Unless it's been towed. "What about transportation?"

"You can take the Bentley."

Holy shit. "Are you serious?"

He chuckles. "Why wouldn't I be serious?"

"Umm... because it's a *Bentley*."

"It's a car, and you have a license to drive. It's not a big deal."

Not a big deal, my ass. "I've seen what happens when I owe you a hundred grand. That car cost a quarter of a million dollars. What will you do to me if something happens to it?"

His mouth stretches into a naughty grin. "I think you know exactly what I'll do to you. And I'll enjoy every second."

This man is obsessed. "You just won't take no for an answer, will you?"

"Taking no for an answer means that I don't get what I

want. Why do that when I can be persistent and eventually get my cock in your ass?"

"Enough already with your anal obsession."

"Let me do it once, and it'll become your obsession too."

I highly doubt that. "Talk about something else, please."

"Your visit to see your family. I want you to be home by six." He sounds like a father giving a curfew to his daughter.

"Yes, Daddy."

"I don't mind hearing you call me that."

I have a father, and it's not Tristan Broussard. "I'm not calling you Daddy."

"You will if I tell you to." He beckons me with his finger. "Come to me, bebelle."

Oh shit. I've fucked up now. He's probably going to spank me.

"Sit on my lap." Sit on his lap instead of lie across it and get my ass blistered? Gladly.

I lower my bottom to sit on his thighs and wrap my arm around his shoulders. "Yes?"

His hand creeps beneath my shirt and dips into the cup of my bra, pulling the material away and exposing my breast for his touch. His thumb and index finger roll my nipple and he pulls on it, making it hard. "Tell Daddy what you want."

"Stop saying that. It's weird."

He pinches my nipple and makes me wince. "I'm just trying it out."

"Well, don't. I don't like it."

He lifts his chin. "Kiss me."

I lean in and place my lips on his. Our mouths open and our tongues move against one another like restless waves.

He twists my nipple, sending an erotic wake-up call to my groin. "Tell Daddy what you want."

The kissing. The breast fondling. The nipple pinching

and twisting. It's turning me on in spite of his calling himself Daddy.

"I want to please you."

"What do you think would please Daddy right now?"

"A blowjob."

"Mmm... I want nothing more than your mouth wrapped around my cock, but a blowjob will cost me another key pull. That would put you at five pulls on the morning of day three. At that rate, you'll pull that key sooner than I want. And I'm nowhere near ready to let you go, bebelle."

He releases my nipple and moves his hand down my stomach, cupping it between my legs over the crotch of my shorts. His mouth devours mine and his hand moves up and down.

His mouth pulls away from mine. "Does baby girl want Daddy to make her come?"

I ignore that creepy baby girl-daddy shit. "Yes, Sir."

"Say it."

"I want you to make me come."

"Finish it."

"Finish what?" I know what he means, but I'm stalling, hoping he'll drop it.

"The sentence. I want you to make me come, *Daddy*. Say it."

I can't do it. "That's what I called my father when I was a little girl, and I still do sometimes. Calling you that is cringeworthy."

"You can't think about it that way; I'm a completely different kind of daddy."

"Well, obviously."

He pushes his hand into the front of my shorts, and the tip of his finger rubs the aching nub at the top of my slit. "I want you to say it, bebelle."

I clear my throat and swallow. "I want you to make me come... *Daddy*." My voice is barely audible when I say the last word.

A deep chuckle rumbles in his chest. "Calling me Daddy doesn't do it for me. Don't say it again."

Thank. Fuck.

Tristan dips his fingers into the sticky ooze between my folds and uses the slick moisture as a lubrication for his fingers to glide over my clit. Side to side. Circles. Up and down. He does a little of everything.

I'm trembling. My breath is rapid. I may even be a little lightheaded. Every nerve ending between my legs is alive. I've never been so desperate to come in all of my life.

He glides his fingers up and down my center. His fingertip grazes my clit with every upward stroke, enough to stimulate but not nearly enough to satisfy. It's torture, the sweetest kind.

I tilt my hips and rock against his fingers. "Please don't edge me, Tristan. I don't think that I can stand it; I need to come. Please."

"Beg for it, bebelle."

I'm not above begging at this point. "Please, Tristan. I need it so badly."

"Louder."

I don't know where Ray is, and I don't care. He knows what Tristan is, and he must know what I am to his employer. "Pleeease, Tristan. I'm in agony. Desperate. Please let me orgasm."

His hand slows and I whimper. Shit. He's going to edge me again.

"Are you desperate enough to let me fuck you in the ass?"

I press my face to his shoulder and shake my head. "I'm desperate but not that desperate."

His finger flicks the sensitive nub a few times. "Will you give me a freebie?"

"A freebie?"

"Give me tonight without a key pull?"

Oh. The jackal wants to weasel out of giving me a key, and he's negotiating the deal at my most vulnerable moment.

"I'll give you vanilla without a key pull, but none of the other stuff. No spanking. No Dom-sub acts. No bossing me around. We make love. You give me what I need, we both come, and I won't ask to pull a key."

He lowers his mouth to my neck, kissing me just below my lobe, and his hand masturbates me into oblivion. "Deal. You may come."

"Omigod." I bite my lip and grasp him tightly around his neck to pull him close.

I tense all over, including my curled toes, when the rhythmic contractions in my groin begin. Once. Twice. I lose count of how many times my internal body squeezes. "Tristan..."

"That's it, bebelle. Ride it out," he whispers against my ear.

I relax when my orgasm ends. My entire body goes lax, and Tristan wraps his arm around my waist to hold me on his lap.

He nibbles my earlobe, sucking it into his mouth. "The way you respond to my touch is sexy as fuck."

"Well, I think that the way you rub me off is sexy as fuck." His hand is so powerful. Mine always gets tired and cramps when I masturbate.

"We have great sexual chemistry, don't you think?"

"We do." Fact. I've never clicked sexually with anyone the way I do with Tristan.

"I need to go to work." He grasps my face and turns it so

our lips are touching, but not kissing. "I'm excited about tonight. I'll think about it all day." He presses a kiss against my lips. "Six o'clock. Don't forget."

"I won't."

～

I DON'T SEE THE NEED IN TAKING A LOT OF MY PERSONAL things to Tristan's house. Seems unnecessary when I could be debt free and back home at any time. But that won't happen tonight, thanks to that stupid orgasm-induced agreement I made with him. I know it was dumb to make that deal, but one freebie won't kill me. It'll be worth it when my toes are curling.

My cash is in the deposit box, and I take one last look around and do a mental check in my head: laptop, iPad, passport, checkbook. I can't think of anything else I should take since Tristan has provided me with everything I'll need.

Most people would be in heaven driving this Bentley, but I'm a wreck. I'm terrified that a rock is going to fly up and crack the windshield or a tourist looking at the beach instead of the road will sideswipe me. My list of potential disasters goes on and on.

I'm relieved when I arrive at Nana's without incident. Until she comes out to meet me in the drive and sees the damn Bentley. "You're driving that bastard's car?"

The way she says *that bastard's car* lets me know that my grandmother isn't in the dark about what's going on. She knows at least a portion of the situation.

Her arms are open for me. "How are you, Nana?"

"Not happy. I've been missing my girl."

"I know. I've missed you, too."

"You've been gone for nine days, sweet pea. Nine. Days.

I've not gone that long without seeing you since you were born."

My mother never wanted to be a mother. She was gone long before she physically left, and Dad didn't know how to care for two little babies. Nana stepped in and took over. She has been more like a mother to me than a grandmother.

"I'm sorry, Nana. I would have come sooner...but things are very complicated."

"I've been worried sick. I wanted to call the police when your father told me that Broussard was forcing you to stay with him. But then he told me the rest of the story—that you were caught. You and Adam both."

"I haven't seen it, but he tells me that he has video surveillance. A lot of it."

"You believe that?"

"Adam and I spent a lot of time in his casino after we started winning. So yes, I do believe him."

Nana's mouth forms a tight puckered O. She hasn't smoked in years, but the lines around her lips formed during her smoking days deepen. "He's a damn bastard just like his father."

"I don't know about his father, but Tristan's not so bad." Anyone who gives me orgasms like he does can't be considered bad.

"He isn't mistreating you?"

Well, I guess most people would regard the spankings and nipple pinching and twisting and orgasm denial as mistreatment, but it doesn't feel that way to me. I don't love the pain, but I sure enjoy the pleasure that accompanies it. It's a fair trade in my eyes. He gets what he wants, and I get what I want.

"He treats me well." Thinking of Tristan in front of my nana makes me blush. "He enjoys spoiling me."

"Is he keeping his hands off of you?"

"Nana, I'm just there as his companion." I hate lying to my grandmother.

"Don't feed me that horseshit like you did your father."

"Nana!"

"Your father believes what you told him about that companion business because he doesn't want to consider the alternative. No father wants to think about any man touching his little girl, but I know better. I'm going to ask you again, and I expect to hear the truth. Is Tristan Broussard keeping his hands off of you?"

Nana is a worldly woman. She isn't stupid and to lie to her after being called out would be an insult to her intelligence. I respect her too much for that. "No, ma'am. He is not."

A murderous expression comes over her face. "Is he forcing himself on you?"

It's difficult to admit to my grandmother that I'm freely giving my body to him. "He hasn't forced me to do anything. I've consented to everything we've done."

"You consented to sex with him because he's threatening to turn over incriminating evidence. That's blackmail. He may not be holding you down and forcing himself upon you, but he has robbed you of your voice to say no. It's just another form of rape."

I don't know why, but I feel the need to defend him. "I could have said no and done the time for my crime, but I didn't. I chose this path with him."

"I can have him taken care of if you want to leave."

Have him taken care of. "What exactly does that mean?"

"I know people who will take him out. Make it look like an accident. All I have to do is give the word."

My nana sounds like some kind of crime boss. "I don't think that a hit on him will be necessary. We're playing a fun little game of chance right now. All of this could be over very soon if fate sees fit for it to be."

"You shouldn't forget that fate can be very cruel sometimes," she says.

"I tell you what, Nana. If I decide that Tristan needs to be taken out, I'll let you know, and you can have him knocked off."

"All you have to do is give me the word and consider it done."

I WALK INTO OUR FAVORITE RESTAURANT AND SEARCH FOR Avery's loose blonde curls; they always stand out in a crowd. Her hand flies up when our eyes make contact, and I wave to let her know that I see her.

It's only been ten days since I last saw her, but it feels like an eternity. Even on the days when we don't see one another, we still text and talk.

"Bitch! Where the fuck have you been?"

I look around to see if anyone is giving us dirty looks. "Could you yell that a little louder? I don't think the family with the three young children over there heard you."

"I'm serious, Em. I've been worried sick. What is going on with you?"

I've been untruthful with Avery about where I've been and why. I didn't feel like my relationship with Tristan was something I could explain to her over the phone. I felt it was necessary for her to see me in person and know that I'm okay before I attempt to weave this tale. "I'm staying in New Orleans with someone."

"You met a man and didn't tell me?" I hear the hurt in her voice and see it on her face.

"No, no. It didn't happen the way you're thinking."

Avery knows how I make a living. I don't have to hide anything about Tristan catching me cheating. And I also don't have to lie about the deal we have or our Dom-sub relationship. "I got caught cheating by the owner of one of the casinos."

Her eyes widen. "Oh shit."

"Oh shit doesn't even begin to cover it, Ave. I was escorted to his private suite in the casino hotel ten nights ago, and he confronted me about the cheating. Long story short, the hundred grand that I not so squarely won at his casino must be paid back. But not with money. My debt can only be repaid with my body."

Avery's hand comes down on the table, making a loud slapping sound. "What. The. Actual. Fuck?"

"I'm pretty sure that I said something quite similar when he made the proposal."

"You have to fuck this guy to pay back the money you won?"

Oh, if it were only that simple. "He wants so much more than sex."

"Like what?"

"Ave..." I lean across the table and so does Avery when she sees that I'm about to spill something juicy. "Tristan is a Dom."

"A Dom?" she yells.

I look around to see if there's anyone in the restaurant who didn't hear her. "Shh."

"A Dom," she whispers. "A real one?"

"I shit you not. He's the real thing."

Avery looks appalled. "Have you been doing kinky stuff with this man?"

"A little bit. I wasn't very keen about it, so he's been introducing the lifestyle slowly."

"What kind of things have you done with him?" she asks.

"He's spanked me a few times. The first time wasn't so bad, but the other times he blistered my ass good."

"Ho... ly... shit."

"He's very alpha and possessive and demanding. I call him Tristan in front of people, but he insists that I call him Sir when it's just the two of us, and he makes me call him Master when we're in the bedroom. Unless he gives me permission to be at ease." I give her a moment to absorb those things. "He also must give me permission to orgasm."

She smiles the second she hears the word orgasm. "He makes you come?"

"Like nothing I've ever felt before. Over and over. It's fucking amazing." Sometimes I think it makes all of this worth it.

"I'm jealous of that part. Every guy I've ever been with was clueless about how to make that happen. What's with that anyway? Don't they learn anything from all of the porn that they watch?"

"All of the guys I've been with before Tristan were clueless too. I don't know what's up with that."

"You said that this guy is demanding? How so?"

"He gives me orders. Stuff like get on your hands and knees. Lie facedown on the bed, ass in the air. Get on your knees and suck my cock. Beg me to allow you to come."

Avery gasps. "You don't feel completely degraded?"

"You'd think so, but it's hot."

"Then he must not be gross?"

"Tristan is older, but definitely one of the hottest men I've ever seen. He's actually sort of beautiful. And the way he turns me on is just downright wrong."

"How old is he?"

"Thirty-six but he looks younger. He's Creole, which gives him an edge that's a little exotic-looking. His hair is dark, and his eyes are the most alluring color of blue. He's so damn handsome. It's the wisps of gray around his face and the bit scattered in his facial scruff that lets you know he's a mature man. That and the designer business suit he's always wearing."

"Whew, I love a man in a good suit."

"As do I."

"Has he hurt you besides the spanking?" she asks.

"He pinches and twists and tugs on my nipples. It hurts, but then it also feels good. I don't really know how else to explain it. It's weird because something about the pain arouses me."

"Is the sex rough?"

"Sometimes but then during other times it's slow and gentle."

"I wouldn't expect a Dom to do slow and gentle."

"He didn't do it with other subs. Just me." I shrug. "I think it's sweet. But then he does a one-eighty and wants to fuck me in the ass. He's obsessed and won't stop talking about it."

"Omigod, Em," she squeals. "Are you going to let him?"

"No! His cock is huge. He barely fits into the kitty door as it is. He'd tear my ass to shreds for sure." I squirm in my seat just thinking about it.

"I bet he knows how to do it the right way so it doesn't hurt."

I can't believe Avery. "Stop taking his side. I don't want to do it."

"I'm not taking his side. I'm just saying that if you're ever going to do it, you'd probably be better off to try it with someone like him who knows what he's doing."

Avery doesn't seem disgusted by the idea of it. "Would you do it?"

"I think I would if I were with the right guy. But that one has yet to come along."

Bless Avery. She has had worse luck with men than I have. Now, that's saying something.

"You think Tristan is the right guy for me? I mean to try that with?"

"Only you know the answer to that."

I wish I could stay and talk longer with Avery, but I spent most of the day with Nana. "I have to go; Tristan wants me to be home by six."

"*Home?*" she asks.

Shit. I did just say that, didn't I? "I'm not referring to his house as my home. Because obviously it's not."

"Didn't sound that way to me. In fact, everything you've told me today sounds as though you're pretty comfortable with him and also with living at his house in New Orleans."

"I'm resigned to doing what I have to do. There's a difference."

"If you say so, Em." I know that grin on her face. She doesn't believe me.

"I do say so."

Avery walks out of the restaurant with me to the parking lot. "How long are you going to be living with him?"

"That's a whole other story." Damn, I can't believe I forgot to tell her about paying back my debt. Or the involuntary IUD placement that led to his new deal. "We originally agreed that I would receive credit toward my debt every time I... satisfied him sexually." It sounds horrible when I say it out loud. "Which makes me a total prostitute."

Avery shakes her head. "That wasn't what I was thinking at all."

"Do I want to know what you're thinking?" Avery is honest. She doesn't beat around the bush, so I'm a little frightened to hear what she has to say.

"I was only thinking that you seem really calm and relaxed, maybe even happy, about being with this man. It seems like you're enjoying your time with him."

I can be honest with Avery about my true feelings. "I'd be lying if I said that I'm not. His lifestyle is new to me, but I like the things that he has done to me. The control, the punishments, the commands... I've never been so turned on by a man in my entire life."

"You never told me how long you'd be there."

"Oh, yeah... my stay is up in the air. We replaced the original repayment method with something different. I blindly pull a key from a box filled with one hundred keys after we engage in his choice of sex. My debt is free and clear when I pull the key that works on a specific padlock. It's basically a game of chance. What can I say? We're both gamblers."

"His idea or yours?" she asks.

"His. It's a deal he came up with to get me to stay."

"I thought you liked what he was doing to you."

"I left off the part of the story where I got abducted and drugged before being transported across the state line to New Orleans. And while I was sedated, I was examined by the OB-GYN who cares for his submissives, and an IUD was inserted into my body without my permission."

"Oh fuck no."

"Oh fuck yes. The bastard is a total control freak. He has to be in charge of everything, and that includes birth control."

"That's some of the craziest shit I've ever heard of."

"I was so pissed off when I found out that I was on my way out the door, freedom be damned. But then he offered this new deal where I could literally clear my debt and any incriminating evidence in a single key pull. I had to take his deal. And I haven't regretted that decision yet."

"I get why you're doing it. I'd have great sex with a hot man to stay out of jail too. I don't know anyone who wouldn't if faced with those two options."

Other women would have judged me and my decision. Probably even slut-shamed me for what I'm doing. But not Avery. And it's only one of the reasons why I love her so much.

"I need to start back. I don't want to be late. Tristan forced me over the dining room table and spanked me the last time I wasn't on time."

"As demented as that sounds, I bet it was hot."

"It was—after I got over the shock of it."

I point to the Bentley. "This is me."

"Whaaat?"

"He kidnapped me, remember? My car isn't at his house in New Orleans, so he had to let me drive one of his."

"He let you borrow a *Bentley*?"

"He's crazy rich."

"Does he have any crazy-rich friends who will kidnap me and force me into submission?"

"Careful what you ask for with a Dom."

6

TRISTAN BROUSSARD

I'm pleased when I see the Bentley in the garage. And relieved. But it has nothing to do with the car. It's been an all-day struggle to suppress my fear of coming home and finding that Emma Lia didn't return.

I don't knock before entering her bedroom. I can't; I'm eager to see her. Anxious to confirm that she is, in fact, here.

I follow the soft sound of music, a romantic and groovy tune by a female singer, and find Emma Lia in the claw-foot tub covered with bubbles to her breasts. She fails to hear me approaching. How do I know? Because she's singing the song at the top of her lungs like no one is standing here listening.

The beautiful girl can't sing worth a damn. It reminds me of terrible karaoke, but her performance is still entertaining.

"Bebelle," I whisper.

She jolts and twists around to look at me in the doorway. "Tristan? You're home? Oh God. I didn't realize that I'd been in the bath so long. What time is it?"

"You're not late. I'm home early."

She places her hands on the rim of the tub. "I'll get out."

"Don't." I slip my jacket from my shoulders. "I want to get in with you."

Tie. Button-down. Shoes. Socks. Belt. Trousers. Boxers. Her eyes watch every piece of clothing come off of my body. She doesn't even try to hide her absorption in watching me get naked.

And I love it. I'm glad she's not timid about her interest in me.

Emma Lia. My little submissive.

The intense satisfaction I feel at that thought is absurd. I sometimes have to remind myself that she's mine only until fate decides that she isn't. But I try to not dwell on it.

I will fuck her and spoil her, and she will satisfy my every desire, no matter how dark and twisted. Mon bebelle will give me every part of herself, and I will devour it. I will take everything that she has to give, and then I will demand more.

But I will give her what she wants tonight: tender, gentle, sweet. The sadistic Dom inside me is satisfied for now and content. I have no desire to bring pain to her tonight. Only to feel her tremble with pleasure in my arms.

My cock is rigid and aching with desire, but the hunger is different from what I usually feel with my submissive. My urge is calm, controlled, composed.

Without my having to ask, Emma Lia scoots forward to make room for me behind her. I step in and lower my body, causing the water and bubbles to rise to her shoulders.

She relaxes against me, her back pressed to my chest, and releases a blissful sigh. After the shit day that I've had, I'm content to sit here with my arms and legs wrapped around her body for a while without saying a word. My brain just needs a fucking break. And as though she senses that need inside of me, she allows my mind to be quiet.

Neither of us move until I lift my hand and stroke my

fingertips over her shoulders peeking out of the bathwater, appreciating her smooth skin, so milky against my darker complexion. My dick aches to move in and out of her, but I'm in no rush. I simply want to enjoy this moment and heighten the anticipation of what's to come.

"Your fingers feel good gliding over my wet skin," she whispers.

I wrap my arm around her body and cup her buoyant breast in my palm. My Dom instinct is to pinch her nipple and pull down while I twist, but instead I gently caress my thumb back and forth over it.

"Mmm... that's nice too."

Giving in to a sudden urge, I place my other hand beneath the water and glide it down her stomach. She parts her thighs and I cup my hand between her legs. The rate of her breathing increases and so does the amount of blood pooling in my dick, making the ache in my groin intensify.

My fingers brush against her pussy, parting her soft lips. I push the tip of my middle finger into her tight opening, using my thumb to massage her sensitive nub at the same time.

Her tight canal is slick and accepts the intrusion of my finger without protest. The inner walls of her pussy close in around my finger, and my cock jerks in response. He wants that tight pussy to hug him, but he'll have to wait his turn.

She moves her hips against my hand, and my finger slides deeper inside her. "Oh, Tristan."

"I love hearing you say my name like that. All breathless and excited and desperate."

She pulls away and tries to reach for my cock behind her back, but I wrap my hand around her waist and pull her toward me, my erection resting against her back.

I press my mouth against her ear. "Just lean against me and relax, bebelle. Enjoy my touch without any thoughts about reciprocation. Think only about my hands on your body and how they make you feel."

I insert a second finger and move both in and out of her at a slow pace, my thumb stroking her clit at the same rate. Her upper body presses against mine and the back of her head falls against my shoulder. She lifts her arm, wrapping her hand around the back of my head. Her face turns toward mine and without any thought at all I press a kiss to the side of her face.

"My beautiful doll." The words slip from my tongue with complete and utter affection. And surprise.

"I'm going to come, Tristan. I can't stop." I hear the doubt in her voice. She's unsure if I want her to come or not.

"Let it happen."

I hear the intense rapture of her orgasm in her moan. Feel it in her body arching against me and the pulsations around my fingers as she comes apart in my arms. So fucking beautiful.

A dozen or so vaginal contractions squeeze my fingers, and then her body relaxes. "No man has ever given me orgasms like you have."

The mention of her being with other men sparks an emotion that I don't care for at all. Makes me want to tell her that she is mine now. That her pussy belongs to me and only me. No other man is to touch it. But I say nothing. That's a discussion for a later time, one that will happen after she sees that she wants to stay and be my submissive beyond the pull of the right key and clearing of her debt.

"I could stay like this all night with you, but we should get out. Ray will be serving dinner soon."

She sits up and scoots forward, allowing me to stand. I reach for the towel she placed next to the tub, but I drop it to the floor when I feel her hand wrap around the base of my dick. "Do you want your cock in my mouth?"

I told her to not think about reciprocation, but damn, my dick is aching for release. "I'm not turning it down if it's what you want to do."

"Just breathe, Tristan. Enjoy my touch. Only think about your cock in my mouth and how good it feels sliding over my tongue and hitting the back of my throat."

Fuck.

Fuck.

Fuuuck.

Emma Lia has a drive to please me. She's already accepting—I mean truly coming to terms with—my role as her Dom even if she doesn't realize that it's happening.

She moves to kneel before me, licks her lips, and grasps the thick base of my erection in her hand. Her mouth hovers over the tip, letting me feel her warm breath on my cock. Letting me anticipate her warm, wet mouth sliding down on it. Putting me on pins and needles. Making me want it so badly that I'll do anything to feel her mouth on me.

She slowly drags her tongue over the tip and then licks every side, base to tip. My whole fucking body convulses when her tongue hits that sensitive spot on the underside of the crown.

I groan when she tilts her chin upward and takes my whole length in—not something every woman is able to do. "Ohhh... fuck, bebelle. I can feel you taking it down your throat and swallowing around the head."

Her head bobs back and forth, her mouth taking my dick in and out. I run my fingers over the back of her hair, petting her. Praising her for a job well done.

She looks up and our eyes make contact. And fuck, she's the prettiest little thing I've ever seen on her knees sucking me off. And the sight of it all ignites the fuse of my orgasm. "Oh fuck. I'm about to come."

She takes my dick out of her mouth. "Give it to me. I want every drop."

She opens her mouth and holds out her tongue, pumping my cock and waiting for me to shoot off into her mouth.

This is the first time that she's sucked me to the point of coming. I'm not sure what I expected her to do, but I don't think it was anything quite this dirty. It just adds to the pleasure she's giving me.

Several white sticky ropes launch into her mouth, and she holds her mouth open, showing me what my cum looks like on top of her tongue. The image definitely competes with watching my cum leak out of her pussy. "Swallow it."

She closes her mouth and her throat slightly bobs. Her mouth opens again and my cum is gone.

I cradle the side of her face with my hand, rubbing my thumb over her mouth. "That was fucking amazing."

She smiles up at me. "I'm glad that you enjoyed it."

"I more than enjoyed that."

I step out of the tub and fetch the towel on the floor before offering her my hand. "Madam."

While gripping her hands, I help her out of the tub and then I wrap the oversized towel around both of us, pressing our wet bodies together. Damn, I love the way her wet breasts feel smashed against my chest.

She looks at me with such fondness in her eyes, as though I've not blackmailed her into being here with me. "What do you want me to wear to dinner?"

"I don't know. Let's go have a look in your closet."

My eyes immediately go to a casual cream-colored sundress, reminding me of vanilla. Very fitting for the rest of the night we're going to have. "I think this will work. Leave your hair in the topknot and skip the makeup with the exception of a peachy-pink lip gloss."

"Yes, Sir."

"I'm not Sir or Master tonight. I'm just Tristan when we're vanilla."

Her eyes alight. "I like calling you Tristan."

I've always preferred Sir in a casual setting, but there's something about hearing Emma Lia say my name that I enjoy. "I like it too."

She rises up on her tiptoes and quickly kisses my mouth. "I'll be down for dinner as soon as I'm dressed."

My immediate thought is that I wouldn't mind her being late to dinner. And then I remember that I can't spank her over the dining room table or anywhere else tonight. But tomorrow is a different story.

Emma Lia is already seated at the table when I come into the dining room. I can't believe that she beat me down here. "Someone was fast."

"It's easy to be fast when all you have to do is put on a dress and lip gloss."

I usually give her a half-hour to get ready for dinner after I direct her on how to look, but she's just as beautiful this way. "Then perhaps I'll have you do that more often."

I take my seat at the head of the table and Ray comes in, placing on the table a plate in front of each of us. "What's on the menu tonight?"

"Shrimp with smoked-Gouda grits."

"One of my favorites. You're going to love this dish, bebelle."

"I'm sure that I will. Looks and smells delicious."

Emma Lia takes a bite and the soft moaning sound that she makes, although triggered by the food, causes my dick to twitch. "Like it?"

"It's incredible." Her tongue darts out to lick her lips. "Mmm... so creamy."

Fuck. I wonder if she knows how damn sexy she is even when simply talking about shrimp and grits.

"I appreciate your returning on time. Did you have a good day?"

She brings her hand to her mouth and covers it when she replies. "It was great. I was thrilled to spend time with my nana and Avery."

"You didn't see Conrad and Adam?"

"They're out of town, but I talk or text with them every day. They check in to make sure that I'm okay."

I figured as much. Conrad and Adam love Emma Lia. There's no way that they'd go without checking up on her.

"Your nana is well?" I ask.

"Better now. She's been worried about me. She was relieved to see for herself that I'm all right."

"I'm glad that her mind has been put at ease."

Emma Lia grins. "Well, I'm not sure that one could say that it's *at ease*. She's pretty put out with you."

"She is, huh?" I can tell that Emma Lia is close to her grandmother by the things that she has told me about her. I can imagine that she would be put out with me.

"Yes." She giggles. "She offered to have you *taken care of*."

"Taken care of as in how?" I know exactly what she means, but I think it will be entertaining to hear her explain.

"Let's just say that she could call in a favor." She lifts a brow. "So you might want to watch yourself, Mr. Broussard."

I was surprised and mesmerized when Emma Lia told me that her grandmother was a casino dealer and also the one who taught Conrad how to gamble and cheat. That made her a very interesting lady in my book, but that was only a scratch on the surface compared to what I've learned about her. "You know, if we were talking about anyone else, I would probably dismiss that statement entirely, but I asked around about your grandmother. I'm not sure if you know this or not, but she has history with the Mafia."

Emma Lia stops eating and looks at me. "What kind of history are we talking about?"

If she doesn't know, it's because her grandmother doesn't want her to know. "I'm not certain that the elder Emma Grant would appreciate my telling her granddaughter about her past."

"Whatever you tell me will be between us. I won't say anything."

"You can't ever mention what I share with you to anyone. One doesn't fuck with the Mafia, bebelle. Not even me."

I have dealings with the Mafia but I'm careful to stay on their good side. We have an understanding that works for both of us, which often includes turning a blind eye to their activities within the walls of my casino. But I'm no saint, and I sleep just fine at night.

"I won't say a word, Tristan. I swear."

"I have some older employees who have been on the casino scene for a while. They remember your grandmother and told me that she was quite the catch back in the day." And I don't doubt that for a moment considering how gorgeous Emma Lia is. "She was beautiful enough to catch the eye of an Italian crime boss. I was told that they were lovers until he was killed."

"Nana has always had a weakness for beautiful Italian men. I'd put my money on that being true."

"You think so?"

She nods. "It wouldn't surprise me, not even a little. Nana is... something else. Not at all a typical grandmother."

"What about your grandfather?"

"They divorced when Dad was a toddler. He went back to Ireland. I've never even met him."

She's Irish. That's where she gets that pale, milky skin that I love so much. Skin that is going to display the red marks of my flogger and crop so well.

Conrad was abandoned by his father. Emma Lia was abandoned by her mother. I see a pattern here, one I'm not unfamiliar with.

"Tell me about your day," she says.

I was chest deep in filth. I hate dealing with gambling addicts. They make life hard for everyone around them. "It was a shitty day, but it got better when I came home and found you in the tub singing your heart out."

She covers her eyes with her hand. "I can't sing for shit."

She sure can't. "Perhaps not, but your attempt was stellar. What were you listening to when I came in?"

"'For Everything a Reason' by Carina Round."

"I enjoyed listening to it while we were in the tub. I'd like you to put on some music like it later."

"You mean when we make love?"

Making love. Damn, that is a term that's going to take some getting used to. Not sure I ever will.

Everything about tonight is for her. But if I'm going to be giving her the vanilla that she wants, I might as well negotiate to get something that I want.

"Will you wear the silk ivory lingerie piece with ruffles and a bow that ties between the breasts?" If we're going to do this sugary-sweet thing tonight then she might as well look the part. And that piece of lingerie is perfect for what I have in mind.

"I'll wear anything you want me to wear."

"Butt plug?"

She giggles. "Clarification: anything but that."

~

I DID SOMETHING TONIGHT THAT I'VE NEVER DONE. Well, I did several somethings that I've never done, but I'm talking about one in particular: reading aloud to Emma Lia.

I found it to be an odd request, but she says that she loves my Cajun accent. Claims it turns her on, so how could I say no when she asked me to read *The Thorn Birds* to her?

I come to a good stopping place, and my cock knows what's going to happen next. The fucker comes to attention at the very moment that I close the book. "Oh, that Father Ralph. He has been a bad boy."

"Are they going to be together one day?"

"It'll ruin the story if I tell you that."

"He loves Meggie, and he's going to leave the priesthood for her. I know he is."

Emma Lia is a romantic. I see it clear as day, so I guess that she would hope for that.

"You'll have to keep reading to find out."

"I told my nana that I was reading the book, and she told me that there is a television miniseries. I checked, and iTunes sells it. I'm planning to watch it after I finish the book, but the damn thing is so freaking old. It came out in the early '80s."

I'm amused that she sees that as ancient. "You are aware that I came out in the early '80s too? In 1982."

She giggles. "I sometimes forget that you're fourteen years older than me."

"Do you consider me old?" I'm thirty-six. That's closer to forty than thirty. I'm pretty sure that I thought that was old when I was her age.

"You're not old to me, Tristan. Not even a little."

She's stretched out on the couch, eyes closed. Her back is propped against the arm of the couch, and her feet are resting on my lap. Her feet are small and pretty, like every other part of her. Sexy even, with the black polish on her toes that has slightly grown away from the cuticle.

I pick up her right foot and apply light circular pressure to her heel. I massage it and delight in the quiet little moans that come from her slightly parted lips. "Mmm... that feels really good."

Surrendering to an unexpected urge, I lift her foot to my mouth and suck her big toe lightly, swirling my tongue around it. She inhales sharply and lifts her head from the arm of the sofa to look at me.

I suck her middle toes and her breathing increases. That's when I realize that this is turning her on. Which turns me on.

Her eyes are on mine when I take her other foot from my lap and give it the same oral treatment. Her toes curl at the touch of my tongue, and her breathing is now panting. Her tongue darts out to lick her lips as she watches my mouth, and blood rushes to fill my cock.

I swear to God that I'm perpetually hard when I'm with this woman.

I return her foot to my lap and slowly glide my hand up her leg beneath her sundress. My fingers reach the inside of her thigh and the muscles there are quivering with tension as I approach that sweet cunt between her legs. And because I want to tease her and also myself, I barely brush the silk fabric of her panties over the outer edge of her pussy lips.

I would fuck her right here and now, but Ray hasn't left for the night yet, and I'm not down with any other man seeing what I consider mine. And then there's also Claudia to consider.

"I think that we should take this to the bedroom."

She nods. "I think so too."

"Go upstairs and put on the ivory chemise without the

panties. And take care of the music. I'll give you a few minutes to get ready, and then I'll come and join you."

"All right."

Emma Lia gets ups and walks toward the staircase. "Bebelle…"

She stops and turns to look at me. "Yes?"

"My bedroom tonight."

She smiles. "Okay."

Longest ten-minute wait of my life. But it's worth every minute when I see Emma Lia sitting on my bed, wearing that sweet, innocent-looking silk gown. She looks like a virginal bride on her wedding night. "Wow. Even more beautiful than I anticipated."

"Thank you."

She watches me as I cross the room. I stop at the bedside and pull my T-shirt over my head. "What song is this?"

"'Just Breathe.'"

The song is slow and easy. Exactly what I think she wants from me tonight. "Who sings it?"

"Benjamin Francis Leftwich."

Her choices in music are interesting to me. Definitely not top-one-hundred chart toppers. "Never heard of him, but I like it."

I kick out of my shoes, drop my jeans and boxer briefs to the floor, and kick them away.

Her bright eyes are hooded with desire as she watches me climb onto the bed between her legs and hover above her soft, tender flesh. I ignore my aching cock and place light kisses on the insides of her thighs, gradually moving up until I reach her pussy.

I spread her folds apart with my fingers and flick my tongue over her clit. She pushes her fingers into the top of my hair and rocks her hips against my mouth. "Ohhh... Tristan... uhhh... that feels sooo good."

Fuck, I love hearing her praise my oral skills.

I push my erect tongue inside her hole, penetrating her as deeply as I can, tasting her essence. I relish every drop that I lap from her body; it's so fucking sweet. Her pussy has the best taste in the world.

She shudders and fists the top of my hair, using her grip to press my face harder between her legs as she rocks against it. I delight in every gasp and moan as my tongue works the sensitive nerves at the peak of her vagina.

She breathes harder, and her thighs tremble on each side of my head. Her hips lift off the bed, and her pussy grinds against my tongue. If those don't confirm her orgasm, the sudden taste of salty-sweet moisture does.

She goes limp, and I crawl up her body. She squirms beneath me as I kiss her body on the way up. "I love everything about your body. It's perfect."

"I am in no way perfect."

"You are to me."

This is the point where I'd normally slide my cock in and pound her tight little pussy until I explode, but not this time. Tonight is for her. I'm going to give her what she asked for.

I'm going to make love to her.

I continue moving up her body and place my mouth over her ear. "You are so sweet, bebelle," I whisper. She shivers and my cock throbs harder, my balls full and aching to fill her with cum, which makes my next words come out low and raspy. "So fucking sweet."

I push the bottom of her gown up, exposing her soft, round breasts. Her rosy nipples are hard, practically begging for my mouth. I close my lips over her taut bud, sucking gently. She massages my scalp with her fingertips and makes a sound that's a cross between a moan and whimper. I give my attention to her other nipple, sucking on it until her body is quaking underneath me.

I release her nipple and move up her body, my chest smoothly gliding against the silk of her bunched gown, until we're face-to-face. My lower arms take the brunt of my weight while I hold myself over her.

Emma Lia's eyes are unfocused, clouded by the blissful aftermath of her orgasm, but they close when I lower my mouth to hers, claiming it with a deep, thorough kiss. Her arms come up and around my neck, her breasts pushing against my chest. Her tongue slides over mine, and I know that she can taste herself on my lips. The thought excites me, making my heart beat a little fast.

Holy fuck. My self-control is fraying.

I have to have her. Now.

I continue to kiss her while I use my knee to spread her thighs and press the head of my cock against her slick opening. I'm so hard that I don't even need my hand as a guide to find where it needs to go.

I stop kissing her and look at her face faintly lit by the bedside lamp. Angelic. Wholesome. Unbroken. She's everything that I've not had in a woman.

"I want you so much, Tristan," she whispers.

I slide my hand into her hair to cradle the back of her head and press a soft kiss to her lips. "I want you too, sweet girl."

Her eyes are on mine when I slowly push into her body. Her slick core accepts me, stretching and lengthening to accommodate my cock. I still when I'm all the way inside her and press my forehead to hers. Slow, I remind myself. You must go slow. For her. It's what she asked for.

Her breath comes in soft little pants against my mouth

when I move in and out. Her legs come up to clasp my hips, the movement bringing me deeper into her, and my dick begs to fuck her into the mattress. But I deny him.

Her arms are wrapped around my upper back and her nails lightly dig into my flesh. "You feel so good inside of me."

"It's so much better than good."

Emma Lia arches against me, her legs wrapping around my body tighter. Every thrust brings me deeper into her until I feel like we're fused and melding into one being. It's a new sensation that I can't give a name to or begin to explain, but I know that she is the reason for it.

She is what I want. She is what I need.

"It's starting. I'm going to come again, Tristan."

Her pussy contracts around my cock several times, and it triggers the climax of my orgasm. "I'm coming with you, bebelle."

She squeezes my body closer using her legs and digs her fingers into the flexed muscles in my ass. "I want all of your cum inside me."

"I'm giving all of it to you, baby."

I move my hand from her head to the back of her neck and use my grasp to hold her in place when I thrust deep, my seed expelling out of my body and into hers. And I'm amazed by how intensely satisfying it is just knowing that she has that part of me inside her.

When our orgasms are over, Emma Lia's hands cradle the sides of my face, and she pulls my face down to hers, pressing a kiss against my lips. "Thank you for that. It was perfect."

I got to have sex with her, and it isn't costing me a key pull. I should be the one thanking her. "I will give you vanilla anytime you want. All you have to do is ask, and I'm happy to oblige."

She smiles. "You aren't going along with this because it's

what I asked for." Her finger pokes against my chest. "Mister... you... *like*... vanilla. You're a Dom who likes making love. What would the friends you have within the lifestyle say about that?"

"They would think that I've lost my mind. Especially Easton." And he wouldn't get finished fucking with me about it if he knew.

"Well, Easton has already proven to me that he's a freak between the sheets. I bet that guy couldn't have vanilla sex if he tried. You, on the other hand, are exceptional at making love."

Because it's still sex. Of course, I'm good at it. How could I not be with this phenomenal dick? But she shouldn't get too used to having it this way.

"Maybe I am, but I couldn't do vanilla all of the time. The Dom inside me must have his release." It isn't pretty when the beast isn't satiated. And he can only be held at bay for so long.

"And I can't do straight-up Dom-sub all of the time. Just as you need to issue commands and punishments to receive gratification, I need to feel tenderness for fulfillment. Even if it isn't associated with love and affection."

"I don't know how to read your cues for what you need. I've not had to do it in a long time, and honestly, I wasn't ever really that good at it anyway. I'm going to need you to help me with that."

She's here to pay a debt. Get me off. I'm not supposed to give two shits if she's getting what she needs from me to be fulfilled or not.

But I'm finding that I do care. I care very much.

"I think that you're doing a wonderful job, but don't worry. You aren't the only one who is good at getting what you want. I'll let you know if I need more from you."

She tightens her legs around me and forces my hips to

thrust against her. The movement forces my softening cock to slip out, the opposite of what she was going for, I think.

She puts her hands against my chest and pushes. "Roll over."

"Why?"

"Just do it and you'll find out."

I know where she's wanting to go with this. "You need to understand something, bebelle. I always top. Always. I don't switch roles."

"You can top when you're in Dom mode, but right now you're in vanilla mode, and I want to be on top."

"Topping isn't about position. It's about who holds the control."

"You always have all of the control, Mr. Bossypants. You know that." She pushes on my chest again. "Get on your back. You'll like what I'm going to do. Promise."

The struggle in my head is a battle between something utterly dark and blindingly bright. The Dom inside me wrestles to hold onto complete control, but the brilliance of her light grows, and the darkness within me fades. I give in to her and the maddening, exasperating desire to give her what she wants.

I concede.

I. Obey. My. Submissive.

And it makes me want to hit the fucking panic button.

Together we turn over and she gets on top on me, her legs spread wide and straddling my groin. I instantly wrap my arms around her hips to regain some control of the situation.

Okay. Maybe this isn't so bad after all. I can handle this.

She flattens her palms against my chest and rubs them up and down my chest. "You have a beautiful body."

"I'm glad you think so. I work hard for it."

"I believe you; no one looks like this without working for it."

She rolls my nipples between her thumb and index fingers and then pinches my nipples, sending a message to my dick, telling it to wake the fuck up. And it does, despite the orgasm I just had.

The "Just Breathe" song ends and the next begins. This one I recognize immediately. "You're a Kings of Leon fan?"

"Yeah. 'Conversation Piece' is my favorite song on this album."

"Agreed. It's a great song."

She lowers her body against mine, and her silky night-gown glides against my skin. Her elbows press into the pillow on each side of my head, and she kisses my mouth. I move my hands to the backs of her thighs and skate them upward until they reach her bare cheeks. I dig my fingers into her fleshy ass and spread her cheeks apart. For a moment, I consider dipping my finger into her slick pussy from behind and then slowly sliding it into her asshole. She'd like it. Hell, she'd love it. I know she would if she'd just give it a chance.

I want her asshole so fucking bad. I'm obsessed with it. And I'm going to have it. But I resist the temptation of trying to get in it tonight. Tonight is about her.

My hands abandon her ass cheeks and move around to her stomach, sliding up her torso beneath the silky fabric. I palm her breasts, her hands cupping over mine, and her nipples harden more beneath my touch.

Her own hands move up her chest to her shoulders, and then to the back of her neck as she rotates her hips, grinding her groin against mine. Reminds me of that scene from *Urban Cowboy* where Sissy rides that mechanical bull like she's fucking it.

She reaches for the bottom of her chemise and pulls it

over her head, tossing it to the floor. She is without one single bit of doubt the most beautiful woman I've ever seen. Everything about her is perfect to me.

She rises to her knees and grips the base of my cock. Somehow, it's hard again, and she positions the tip at her warm entrance, drenching wet with the mixture of her pussy juices and my cum. Her body sinks down slowly, and my cock slips into her until I'm buried balls deep inside her. She leans back, placing her hands on my thighs for support, and begins moving up and down in a slow, deliberate rhythm. And fuck, it feels fantastic.

I haven't had sex in this position since I was in my early twenties. That's when I became a Dom. I got my first taste of ultimate control over another person in the bedroom, and there was no way that I was going to relinquish that control.

Until now with Emma Lia.

Unbelievable. Mon bebelle asks and I cave to her after almost no argument.

I thought that I was craving an unbroken woman because I wanted to be her first Dom and train her to my particular tastes. But maybe that isn't the only reason. Is it possible that my craving is a need for something other than dominance and submission? Something... *normal*?

Normal. I hate that fucking word so much.

I don't know what's happening to me. The only thing that I know for sure right now is that Emma Lia's pussy feels like heaven around my cock.

Her hands leave my thighs, and she leans forward, her palms flattened on my chest, and I regret telling her to keep her hair up. I want to see her gorgeous chestnut locks cascading down her shoulders.

"Take your hair down for me."

She doesn't hesitate to reach up and remove the fastener

holding her topknot in place. When her hair falls down, she pushes her fingers in at the roots and fluffs it out.

"You are so fucking beautiful."

She leans forward, lowering her head enough for the ends of her hair to tickle my chest, and slowly rides my cock up and down. I groan with pleasure and grasp her ass, spreading her cheeks apart, as I begin thrusting upward to meet her stroke for stroke.

"Can you come like this?" I ask.

"Not without some help."

I rotate my hand, palm side up, and slide my hand between us until my fingers find her clit. I start with a slow, spiraling motion and increase the speed as she moves faster. I rub it in no particular order. Fast. Slow. Soft. Hard. Her closed rosebud mouth blooms and becomes a helpless O of pleasure. And I know when her breathing picks up that she's catching up with me.

She sinks deeper and groans, "I'm going to come, Tristan. Right now."

I feel the ripple of her body tightening around my cock, and then it's over for me. I explode inside her again, grabbing her hips, bringing her down hard on my cock as I thrust upward. I hold her in place as I spasm, completely emptying myself into her again.

When it ends, she places her hands on each side of my face and presses a soft kiss against my mouth.

"Bebelle, I'm breaking a lot of my own rules for you."

She giggles and presses another kiss to my mouth before moving to lie next to me. "Yes, I suppose you are. But isn't it so much fun?"

She nestles beside me, her head on my shoulder and one leg tossed across mine. Her finger traces circles in the hair on my chest. Cuddling.

Fuck, I've never cuddled. Not even before I became a Dom.

Before I was a Dom, I was an asshole. I immediately left after sex, and since becoming a Dom, I've always sent my submissive away once I was satisfied. Because when the sex is over, that's the point when I'm finished with a woman. But I don't feel finished with Emma Lia. And I don't want to spend the rest of the night apart from her. "I want you to stay with me."

I panic a little after I say the words, afraid that she might think my invitation to stay means that our D/s relationship has changed. It hasn't. "Just for tonight and then things go back to the way they were," I quickly add.

She stops tracing circles on my chest and pulls away. "I can go to my room now if my being in your bed freaks you out."

Shit. I think that I've pissed her off.

"Everything about tonight is vanilla, and that means sleeping together afterward." Lie. The truth is that I want her next to me.

She stares at me for a moment. "I don't know if I want to stay."

Fuck, I'm surprised by how much I dislike hearing her say that.

I grasp her arm and pull her down to lie on my chest again. "You're staying, bebelle."

She relaxes against me, returning to her previous position. I wrap my arm around her and pull her close, caressing her shoulder with my fingertips. And then my peripheral vision catches movement across the room.

Claudia. She's standing in the doorway between my room and Emma Lia's. Watching us.

How long has she been there? Did she watch us fu... make love?

My cutting glare is a warning. My signal for Claudia to leave immediately without making her presence known to Emma Lia. Mon bebelle would freak out if she knew we were being watched by anyone, especially Claudia.

"My throat is dry. I'm going to get a drink. Do you want me to bring back anything for you?"

"I'm fine, thanks."

I get up and drag on a T-shirt and sleep pants. Which pisses me the fuck off. I was exactly where and how I wanted to be for the rest of the night.

I close my bedroom door on my way into the hall; I don't want Emma Lia to hear the sound of our voices carrying down the hallway. I'm furious, and things could become heated.

Claudia is standing at the door of her bedroom when I ascend the stairs. "I can't believe you, Tristan."

I grab her upper arm and shove her into her room, closing the door behind us. "What the fuck was that about?"

She yanks her arm away from my grasp. "I could ask you the same."

How dare she act as though she has the right to question anything I do. "No, you can't because what I do with my submissive is my business. Not yours."

"Are you fucking kidding me? You call that cunt a submissive?"

"Watch it, Claudia."

"Or what? You'll punish me?" She holds up one of my belts and takes my hand, forcing it open and placing it in my palm. "Take it. Punish me, Master. I've been bad."

She slips her robe off and crawls onto the bed on all fours. She's wearing my once-favorite black teddy. And I feel nothing.

Absolutely nothing.

The belt makes a thud when it drops onto the wood flooring. "No, Claudia. You're not my submissive anymore."

She lowers her head and upper body, her ass in the air. "We both need this, and you know it."

"You may, but I don't."

She pushes her fingers under the edge of the teddy at her hip and follows it until she reaches the G-string strap in her cleft. She pulls the fabric to the side and pushes her finger into her asshole. "You want to fuck me in the ass. I know that you do. And I'll let you do it right now as hard as you want. Your little girlfriend won't."

It's not Claudia's asshole that I yearn to have.

"Stop this. Now. We are over, and it's time for you to find another Dom to satisfy your needs. Immediately."

Claudia takes her finger out of her ass and lets go of the fabric before turning over and lying on her back. "You fucked her face-to-face, Tristan. Made her come three times. Three. Times. You never did those things with me. Do you have any idea how much it hurts to see you do that with her?"

"She is my submissive, and I'm with *her* now. I will do whatever I want to do with her. And let me point out that you wouldn't have been hurt if you hadn't been watching us. You had no right to do that."

Claudia rises and props on her elbows. "You're out of your mind if you think she is a submissive. She doesn't have what it takes, and she never will."

"This lifestyle is brand new to her, and she's adjusting beautifully."

Claudia laughs. "It looked to me like you were the one adjusting for her."

"You know what, Claudia? I am adjusting for her, and I

fucking love everything we've done. I don't need to hurt her to be satisfied. *She* makes me happy. *Her*. She is enough for me."

"For now, but it's only temporary. She's your shiny new toy, but guess what? The shine will wear off and when it does, all you're going to have is a plain old ordinary girl. There's nothing special about her."

"Maybe so, but until that time I'm going to enjoy what I have with her."

She rises to a sitting position. "I'm here for you, Tristan. When you're tired of vanilla, I'm here."

Wrong. She isn't going to be here, which reminds me of the meeting I set up for her. "How did it go with Jacob last night?"

"I didn't go."

Oh hell no. "You better be fucking kidding me."

"Do I look like I'm kidding?"

I went to a lot of trouble to meet with him and set up that appointment. Plus, it makes me look like a weak-ass Dom because she didn't show. "I can't fucking believe you, Claudia."

"And I can't believe that you think I would go; you know that you're the only Dom I want."

I can see that she can't be reasoned with right now. "I'm done with this conversation."

She launches from the bed and wraps her arms around me. "Please don't go back to her."

I peel her arms off my body. "Find a new Dom. Soon. I need you out of my house."

Claudia has never been so obstinate. It would have served her well to have exercised some of that disobedience when she was my submissive. I might not have become so bored with her.

But it's too late now.

7

EMMA LIA GRANT

Last night was sooo good. I could get hooked on that kind of sex with Tristan, but I know that vanilla doesn't fulfill him the way it does me.

The man needs to fuck. Needs to be rough. Needs to cause pain.

I wish that he weren't that way. But he is, and there's nothing I can do about it except be grateful for the times when he is gentle with me.

I stretch and open my eyes, finding that Tristan is still next to me, awake and smiling. That's a good sign that he isn't freaking about my being in his bed.

"Good morning, sunshine," he says.

"Good morning."

He twists and reaches for something on the nightstand. He turns back to face me and places an elegantly wrapped gift from a high-end luxury jeweler on the bed beside me. "I have a gift for you."

"What kind of gift?"

"Let's call it a *you-are-my-submissive-and-I'm-going-to-spoil-you* gift."

"Ooh, I like the sound of that."

My mouth feels dry and sticky. I was probably mouth breathing and maybe even snoring, according to what Tristan has told me, so I know my breath can't be pleasant. "Give me a minute to freshen up. Be right back."

After dashing to my bathroom, I brush my teeth and comb my hair before rushing back to bed, eager to open my gift from Tristan. "Hmm… I wonder what in the world this could be."

I tear away the ribbon and rip the paper. My heart speeds a little because I've never been given a piece of jewelry by a man other than my dad. The guys that I've dated in the past have been closer to my age and not financially stable enough to afford even an inexpensive piece of jewelry from a store like this one.

I crack open the box, and it's a matching set that includes a necklace, earrings, and bracelet. Very posh. Very formal. Very expensive.

I finger the center stone of the necklace. I don't even know how many carats it would be, but it's huge. "Tristan… this is beautiful, but it's so formal. I have no idea where I'd wear it."

"I have a business trip, and you're going with me. We fly out in the morning."

"Where to?"

"Destination Vegas. And you're going to wear this set of jewelry to a high-stakes poker game that we'll be attending."

Omigod. I'm going to Las Vegas with Tristan Broussard. He'll rub elbows with important people while we're there. Being seen with him only builds my image within the casino world. No one in their right mind would think that he's keeping the company of a professional gambling cheat.

This is a good thing. Perfect, actually.

I hurl myself onto his lap, my arms wrapped tightly around his shoulders. I bury my face in the side of his neck and squeeze him tightly. "There's no one else in this world I'd rather go to Vegas with. Thank you. For the trip and the jewelry."

"I told you that I was going to spoil you, bebelle. This is only a small taste."

I release my hold on him. "You said that this trip is business?"

"It's always been a dream of mine to have my own casino, one that I've overseen from the ground up. Not one that I've inherited from my grandfather. And I'm going to make it happen."

"Fuck, Tristan. That's a huge undertaking."

"Language, bebelle. Or you know what will happen."

Yes, I do. And I'm sure he'd like nothing more than to punish me, but I'm not ready to go there just yet. Not after the wonderful night we just had.

When we were making love last night, I had a fleeting thought that there was something more to Tristan. Until he told me that things would return to the way they were. That's when I realized that I was only getting one night in his bed. And I remembered what he is and what I am to him—a pretend submissive who's working off a debt to him.

His words hurt me. Made me feel insignificant.

I don't want to think about that anymore.

"How long is this Vegas getaway?"

"A week. Everything is still in the early stages, so I'll be attending a lot of meetings. This trip is going to be all business for me. You'll be free to do as you like as long as you're available to me when I want you."

Available to talk. To fuck. To suck his dick. Whatever he needs in the moment. He doesn't have to say the words. I already know that my duties in Vegas won't differ from what they are here in New Orleans. I'm his to do with as he pleases.

"What time is our flight?"

"I chartered a private jet. We're scheduled to leave at seven in the morning."

"I guess I'll spend today packing."

"Elizabeth will be bringing over some new clothes for you to try on."

"Do I get to choose?"

"If you like. But I've already chosen the lingerie that you'll be taking to wear for me." He grins. "I want us to explore our Dom-sub relationship on a much deeper level while we're on this trip. You should expect many new things."

New experiences with Tristan. That's exciting and frightening as fuck at the same time.

"We have a reservation under Broussard."

The clerk's nails click against the keyboard as she types his name. "Tristan Broussard? Seven-night stay in the presidential suite?"

"Correct."

No surprise there. Of course, Tristan booked the best room that this casino has.

"Wonderful. It'll only take a moment to get you checked in, Mr. and Mrs. Broussard."

I don't fail to pick up on the twitch of Tristan's hand resting on the counter or the minuscule lift at each side of his mouth when the clerk calls me Mrs. Broussard. "Thank you. My wife and I would appreciate a speedy check-in. We had an early flight, and we're both very tired."

The pull at the corners of his mouth tug a little harder when he looks at me. "Isn't that right, Mrs. Broussard?"

Okay. I can play this game if he likes. "Yes. I would love to lie down before we go out."

The bellhop loads our bags onto the cart, and we follow him to the elevators. "I guess that you're used to your subs being mistaken for your wife," I whisper.

"That's actually the first time it's ever happened; you're the first sub that I've brought on one of my trips."

"Really?" I assumed that he took all of his subs with him since he told me in the beginning that he would be taking me on his business trips.

"Our relationship is new. I wasn't ready to be apart from you." He lowers his voice. "I have a lot of new things that I want to do to you. I wasn't willing to wait a week."

Oh shit.

"Do you remember your safe word?"

"Rouge," I answer.

"I gave you a safe word to use if you can't handle what I'm going to do to you. Don't forget it."

The suite is enormous, the decor extravagant with no shortage of luxurious furnishings in shades of gold and taupe. The bathroom is majestic in matching tones. My mouth may drop a little when I see the enormous shower with a gazillion faucet heads and a gigantic jetted tub the size of a small swimming pool. I get a little tingly between my legs when I think about Tristan getting into the tub with me like he did at home last night.

At home. There are those two damn words again.

His house is not my home. So stop saying that as though it is, Emma Lia.

"This is amazing, Tristan."

"I thought you might like it."

"Have you stayed here before?"

"Many times."

I go to the floor-to-ceiling windows and look out over the strip. Seeing the strip of casinos just does something to me. "I love this view."

"Good. You can admire it while I fuck you from behind." I turn and look over my shoulder, and Tristan is advancing toward me, tugging at his necktie. "I'm going to fuck you right now, against the window, completely naked, so anyone who's looking can watch us."

Ohhh fuck.

"I'm taking off your clothes, *Mrs. Broussard*."

I'm so stunned by his words that I can't move. Can't speak. Can't think.

He reaches me, grips the top of my sheath dress's zipper, and pulls it down slowly. His mouth covers my ear, his warm breath sending chills down my body. "The heels stay on, Mrs. Broussard."

"Should I call you Master? Or Mr. Broussard?"

"I like Mr. Broussard for this scene."

He pushes my dress down my body and it falls into a puddle on the floor. I lift one foot and then another, kicking it away. My bra goes next and he drags my G-string down my legs. I'm left in only my heels and jewelry.

"Hands on the window and spread your feet apart." I do as he says and he strikes my right cheek with his palm. Hard. It's definitely going to leave a reddened handprint. "Farther apart, Mrs. Broussard. I'll never be able to fit my enormous cock inside you like that."

The urge to smile is overwhelming, and it wins out.

"Yes, Mr. Broussard."

He strikes my left cheek. "Is something funny, Mrs. Broussard?"

The sting is enough to wipe away any trace of my grin. "No, Mr. Broussard. Nothing is funny."

His body pushes against mine, forcing my upper forehead and chest to press against the window's glass. And mother-fucker... it's cold. My nipples painfully harden to points that could possibly cut through the glass like diamonds.

My jaw clenches and I suck air through my gnashed teeth. "Ooh... ooh... ooh."

His chuckle is low and throaty. Bastard. He knows exactly what he's doing to me, and he's enjoying the fuck out of it.

He nibbles my earlobe and then his mouth hovers over the shell of my ear. "Does Mrs. Broussard want her pussy to be licked?"

A completely different kind of chill spreads over my body. "Yes."

"Beg for it."

I've figured out this game. Plead a little and then plead a little more until I'm downright begging. Let him know that he's the one in charge and that I'm at his mercy. My orgasm is completely and utterly at his discretion, and I will only come with his permission.

"Please lick my pussy, Mr. Broussard."

"Tsk... tsk, Mrs. Broussard. Not good enough."

"Pleeease. I want your mouth on my pussy sooo baaad."

"Better, but not loud enough."

I raise my voice per his request. "Please, Mr. Broussard. I'm begging you to lick my pussy. I'm at your mercy. I can't even tell you how much I want and need your talented tongue. You're the only one who can make me feel good."

"Good girl," he whispers, satisfaction oozing in his tone.

He goes down on his knees behind me and spreads my cheeks apart. "Tilt that beautiful ass up for your husband."

I lean against the cold window and arch my lower back, not allowing myself to think about this little game of husband and wife too much.

"Oh, that's my good girl."

He spreads my cheeks and pushes his face against my pussy, licking it from front to back in one long stroke, making my knees weak. This is going to be so fucking good. I can already tell.

His tongue laps at my lips, my center, and then his tongue moves from front to back without stopping.

Whoa. Wait.

Did he just lick my asshole? On purpose?

I must have relaxed too much, and he must have become overzealous. Because I don't think that he would intentionally do something like that.

I deepen the arch of my back so he can have more pussy and less asshole.

"Feels good?"

"God, yes."

"Want me to stop?"

"Never."

His tongue flattens against my pussy lips and he slowly drags it down... and then up again over my asshole a second time.

Is he getting confused about my anatomy because we're in this awkward position? Should I say something? No, that will kill the mood for him entirely. Hell, worrying about it is sort of killing the mood for me. This is hot. I need to just go with this.

He spreads my slit and pushes his tongue into my pussy. My muscles clench and relax in an effort to build my orgasm.

Tristan tongue fucks me and then shakes his face against my body, making my cheeks shake violently. "Fuck, I love your pussy so much."

I've never had a man seem so obsessed with my vagina. He acts like he's never had better, which is a complete turn-on for me.

"I love your mouth on my pussy."

His arm stretches around my body and his fingers rub my clit as his tongue glides up and down my pussy lips. My orgasm is climbing and building and growing. And I don't know if he's going to give me permission to come or not. "I can feel it starting. I'm going to come."

His fingers continue rubbing my clit, but his tongue abandons my pussy and moves to my tight puckered hole. He flattens it and moves his head up and down, licking it.

And it feels so damn good.

But why? It's not intended for that. It shouldn't feel this way.

My back arches and I tense when the quivering begins in my pussy. He pushes his tongue against me harder and it's almost more than I can stand. "Ohh... I'm coming so hard."

My body shudders and my womb flutters in a rhythmic pattern. A pulsating warmth spreads through my body. Everything tingles—my face, my hands, my feet. And my ears are ringing.

While he licks me... *there*.

This is so wrong.

I spiral down from the high and relax against the glass, now relieved by its cool temperature.

I hear him kick off his shoes, and I don't dare to turn around and look when I hear small thuds on the padded carpet behind me, but I count them. One, his jacket. Two, his tie. Three, his shirt. Four, his pants and belt.

Tristan's front presses against my back, his hard cock probing at my entrance. "Arch your back so I can slide my cock in, Mrs. Broussard."

I rest my upper body against the glass window and use all of my strength to tilt my ass up so Tristan can fit his fat cock inside me. When I'm in position, it slides through my slick folds into my pussy.

"Mmm." He wraps his arm around my waist and holds me tightly. "Only someone I call wife can withstand the fuck session I'm about to give you."

The first brutal thrust is delivered and nearly lifts me out of my heels. "Uhh!"

Tristan pounds his cock into me without mercy. Every thrust is solid because there's no cushion from a bed or couch. "You can scream if you want to, Mrs. Broussard. Cry even. I love both."

The room is filled with three sounds: Tristan's brutal grunts, my ardent squeals, and the wet suction-friction sound of his cock rapidly jackhammering into me. My entire body is being jarred because he's fucking me so hard.

He fucks me that way until my body quivers with exhaustion. A veil of sweat has formed over both of us and our skin is now sliding against one another with hardly any friction. I'm even having trouble holding my palms and forehead against the window; they keep sliding.

Tristan's hands grip the backs of my thighs, and he lifts me like a chair against his chest, carrying me to the bedroom. He tosses me onto the bed facedown and crawls over me, his cock slamming into me before I can get situated. "Take it, Mrs. Broussard. Take every inch with your ass up and your head down."

Every thrust feels like he's touching something deep within me. I don't know what, but it's tender. Not unbearable, but I can't stop the scream that expels from my lungs each time he hits it. And my screams only manage to jockey him on.

He pulls out of me. "Get on your back."

I muster all of my remaining strength to flip over. He

kneels between my thighs and jerks on his cock, his face contorted. "I'm close, Mrs. Broussard."

"Come on me, Mr. Broussard."

He closes his eyes and jerks faster.

"I'm your wife, Mr. Broussard. Mark me. Claim me. Show me that I'm yours."

I don't even know where those words came from. It's like they formed on their own and tumbled from my mouth.

Tristan lowers his body to hover over mine. He holds his weight above me with one arm, forcing every muscle in his arm to bulge. So fucking sexy.

He squeezes his eyes closed for a second and groans. And then opens his eyes wide and watches stream after stream of cum shoot from the tip of his cock landing on my stomach, my chest, my neck, my chin, my face. "Tell me who you belong to."

"I belong to you."

He releases his grip on his cock and places his flat palm on my chest. He slides it through the cum, smearing it all over me. Rubbing it into my skin. "Mine."

I put my hand on top of his. "Yours."

His arm is shaking violently, but he lowers his face to mine and places a soft kiss against my lips before rolling to his back and collapsing.

His breath is a pant, as is mine. And as I work to catch my breath, I reflect on what just happened.

Fuck, that was intense.

Fuck, that was weird.

We just spent the last twenty minutes pretending to be a married couple who fucks like savages. I don't even know what that was all about. And I'm afraid to ask.

Tristan lifts my hand and brings it to his mouth, placing a

soft kiss on the top. A complete contradiction of what he just did to me. "Come here."

I roll toward him and assume the same cuddling position as last night. He glances down at me. "Everything okay?"

"Yeah."

"Sure? That was pretty intense."

"I'm good."

He rubs his hand up and down my arm. "I've never done anything like that—I mean the husband-and-wife scene."

A giggle forms in my chest and rises to leave my mouth. "Me either."

"I liked it. I'll probably want to do it again."

Pretending like that was a little weird, but hot. I didn't mind. "Whatever you want, Mr. Broussard."

"I was thinking we could have dinner at one of the hotel restaurants and then turn in early. I have an early meeting."

It's been an exhausting day. We were up at four this morning, and then our chartered flight was delayed for some reason. Tristan wasn't a happy man. "I think that's an excellent idea."

"We'll unpack our things when we get up and then go out for an early dinner."

I touch the cum between my breasts. "I can't go to dinner without a shower."

"What about a bath together? After a short nap?"

"That sounds perfect."

Tristan chooses a floral halter dress for me to wear to dinner. Soft. Flowing. Romantic. Elizabeth did a great job of choosing clothes for me. I don't think that I could have picked anything that I liked better.

Tristan is on the sofa waiting when I come out of the bathroom. "Sorry. Didn't mean to take so long."

He looks at me, and I don't mistake the long breath he inhales before slowly exhaling. "Worth. Every. Minute. You look beautiful."

I never tire of hearing Tristan tell me I'm beautiful. "Thank you."

"Don't forget your ID."

I giggle because I always get carded for drinks and at the entrance into a casino. "Right."

I'm a bit on the small side for a grown woman. And I have a young-looking face with big eyes and a pixie nose. I'll give them that, but I have boobs and hips. My body has the shape of a grown woman.

Despite the early hour, the restaurant is already pretty crowded when we arrive. People are standing around, waiting to be seated. "Looks like everyone else had the same idea as us."

Tristan grins when he sees the hostess. "Let me handle this."

"Go for it." I stand back and let the man who gets what he wants go to work.

I stand next to Tristan at the hostess's stand waiting to see how he handles this situation. "Hello. Welcome to Flannigan's."

"Good evening. The name is Broussard, and we need a table for two. No. I guess it's a table for three now. Isn't it, honey?" Tristan puts his arm around me, pulls me close, and places his hand on my stomach. "We just found out that we're having a baby. Like literally thirty minutes ago when she took the test in the hotel room. We've been trying for three years, and it finally happened. I'm sorry. That was probably too much information, but we're just so thrilled."

"Congratulations. That is wonderful," the hostess says.

"I was hoping we could have a romantic dinner to celebrate, but you look really busy."

The hostess smiles and winks. "Let me see what I can do to help you celebrate your little miracle."

Tristan smirks and winks at me. So damn smug. And I'm not the least bit shocked when the woman returns to escort us to a table. "Enjoy your dinner, and congratulations again on your little bundle of joy."

"A baby? Wow. Just... wow." He played on that woman's emotions like it was nothing.

"Don't act so surprised. I believe that you're the one who called me ruthless."

Yes, I did. Because there are no bounds that this man won't cross to get what he wants.

Ruthless bastard.

I STRETCH, AND MY MUSCLES SCREAM IN AGONY, reminding me of the rough fucking that I took from Tristan yesterday. Damn, the man was a beast. So much so that I must literally take some oral pain reliever for my sore muscles and stiff joints today.

We didn't have sex last night after we went to bed. We lay down, talked for a little while, and then turned off the lamps and went to sleep. I didn't hate that. My pussy took a pounding and was still sore after soaking in the tub.

Tristan comes out of the bathroom and sits on the bed beside me, his hand behind his back. "Good morning."

"Good morning."

"I have to go; my meeting is in thirty minutes."

"Will you be gone all day?"

"I will. This morning's meeting is only the first of three I have scheduled for today."

That's disappointing. "I won't see you until tonight?"

"No. You're completely on your own today, but you do have an appointment at eleven."

"What kind of appointment?"

"A little bit of well-deserved pampering. I scheduled you for an hour and a half in the spa, and then an hour with a masseuse—a woman, per my request. I don't want any man to put his hands on my submissive."

Tristan confuses me. He allowed Easton to fuck Claudia while she was his submissive, but he won't even let a male masseur touch me for a massage. His possessive alpha-male tendencies toward me are unexpected.

I stretch a bit. "A massage will be wonderful. I'm super sore from that wild fuck yesterday."

He smiles. "The wild fucks have only just begun, bebelle."

"I'm bebelle again?"

"You're always bebelle."

I like being bebelle, but I also liked being Mrs. Broussard yesterday.

"Would you like to do another scene like that? Be Mrs. Broussard?"

"Only if it's what you want." Lie. I'm dying to do it again. I want to strip off his suit and do it right now.

"I would like to do it again." He pushes his hand below the sheet and rubs my butt cheek. "I also have other things that I want to do to you."

I sense something anal-related. "Like what?"

"Can't tell you. Gotta show you."

Maybe he isn't referring to anal sex. He never hesitates to tell me that that's what he wants. "When?"

"Tonight."

Good. Hopefully my soreness should be worked out by tonight. "Look forward to it."

He leans down, presses a closed-mouth kiss to my lips, and digs his fingers into the flesh on my ass. "Have a fun day."

"I will."

"I'll text when I'm finished with my meetings, and we'll have dinner together."

"Do you want to choose my outfit now so I can be dressed and ready to go when you finish with your meetings?"

He looks thoughtful for a moment. "Wear the royal blue dress. Hair down in loose curls. Nighttime makeup that will go well with the dress."

"As you wish."

He moves his hand from behind his back, and I see why he was keeping it out of my sight. "I'm going to use this on you tonight."

Shit.

Strips of leather attached to a leather braided handle. All black. The thing screams pain. And ecstasy.

He drags the leather tails of the flogger over my thighs. "We both have all day to think about it."

I'm tempted to ask him to hit me with it now, so I won't spend the day worrying about it. The words are on the tip of my tongue, but I can't bring myself to say them.

"I'm very excited about taking our relationship to this next level. How are you feeling about it?"

"Scared."

"I understand, bebelle. But I'm not going to do anything to you that you can't handle. Ever. All you have to say is rouge, and it ends right then and there. I swear this to you."

I look at the flogger in his hand. "What if I can't handle it?"

"We'll start out slowly, and you can tell me what's okay and what's not. I will listen and honor whatever you say."

I nod. "All right." I want to tell him that I trust him. I know that's something that is very important to him, but I'm not there yet.

Tristan leans down and kisses my forehead, and it feels so affectionate. "I will see you this evening."

"All right."

"Enjoy your massage and spa day."

As if there's a chance I wouldn't. "I have a feeling that I will."

An affectionate kiss on the forehead this morning.

An ass-whipping tonight.

I need a massage because the man gives me whiplash.

The door shuts and I pick up the flogger. I drag the leather strips over the palm of my hand and know exactly what I have to do if I'm to have any peace of mind today.

I lift the flogger and bring it down as hard as I can on my thigh. The leather strips sting my skin, but it's tolerable. Maybe even pleasurable in a weird kind of way, but I already know that there will be a lot more velocity behind it when Tristan uses it on me.

Maybe he'll let me be Mrs. Broussard again.

I ENTER THE SPA AND THE RECEPTIONIST HEADS ME OFF before I can say a word. "Mrs. Broussard?"

Well, well. It looks like I am Mrs. Broussard. "Yes."

"We're ready for you. Right this way."

I follow the small brunette into a room at the back of the spa. She places a luxurious robe on the chair and instructs me on what we'll be doing. Once changed, I'm taken to a private room where the magic begins.

I'm mannied, peddied, scrubbed, and buffed to perfection. My time ends too soon but then I'm moved to another room where I'm instructed to lie facedown on a table, draped only across my butt.

The next hour flies entirely too quickly, but I'm feeling refreshed and relaxed when I leave. I almost forget entirely that I'm going to get flogged in a few hours. Almost.

I walk by several shops in our hotel lobby as I'm walking toward the elevator and something in the window of a shop catches my eye.

A showgirl costume. And it is magnificent.

The black bustier is trimmed in scarlet red with a bow sitting directly between the breasts. Black and red feathers form a skirt across the back and it has a small matching headpiece. The look on the mannequin has been completed with black fishnet stockings.

Hot. Hot. Hot.

Tristan says that I'm to never wear lingerie that he hasn't chosen, but I think any man would love this. Plus, it's a costume. It can't be considered lingerie.

The urge to wear it for him is overwhelming. I don't think that I can resist buying it and surprising him by dressing as a burlesque showgirl.

When in Vegas...

Tristan is a Dom. No one could be more open-minded when it comes to sexual role-playing. Isn't that what we did yesterday when we pretended to be husband and wife?

I enter the boutique for a closer look at the burlesque outfit, and a saleswoman is by my side immediately, asking how she can help me. "How much is the burlesque costume?"

"Two thousand dollars and worth every penny. It's one of

a kind, and I assure you that the craftsmanship is excellent. Isn't it beautiful?"

Shit! Two grand for that tiny little outfit? I'm not a tight ass when it comes to spending some money, but that seems excessive to me for a bustier and feathers.

But it is gorgeous. And I think Tristan would love it. I bet none of his other submissives have ever shown up in the bedroom in something like this. "I'll take it."

I WALK OUT OF THE BEDROOM INTO THE LIVING ROOM, and Tristan is talking to someone on his cell. Sounds like a business call. "That's not acceptable. I'm only in Vegas until next Sunday."

Tristan takes notice of me and inspects me from head to toe. He winks and mouths, "Beautiful."

I mouth, "Thank you."

He motions with his hand for me to join him on the couch. He inspects my nails and removes my fuck-me pumps so he can see my toes. I giggle when he brings my foot to his mouth and sucks my big toe, all while never missing a beat as he talks business.

If this leads to where it did last time he sucked my toes, I'm going to be on my back getting fucked when he ends this call. And that can't happen. I want to save it all for tonight when I'm wearing my surprise for him.

He gives me those eyes—the ones that tell me he wants to do something very dirty as soon as he finishes this call. I shake my head from side to side and mouth, "No."

Lifting his brows, he counters with a slow nod and look of determination. "Yes."

"No," I whisper. "There will be none of that until later."

I'm certain that he'll hate being told no, but he's just going to have to not like it because I want to save all of the fun for tonight. I want his anticipation to be at its highest.

"That sounds good, Trevor. I'll call you in a couple of days, and we'll discuss it further."

I suspect that he's ending his call sooner than he would have because of my rejection. "And just why not?"

"I have something special for you later, and fucking right now will ruin it."

"Fucking never ruins anything. It makes everything better."

I sigh loudly. Dramatically. "We're not doing it right now. You're waiting until after dinner. Sorry."

"I've never been told no by my submissive."

I don't think that this man has heard no many times in any part of his life. It might do him some good. "Well, this sub is telling you no."

"I don't like it worth a fuck." He's sullen, but I swear that he's still hotter than hot.

"It's going to be so damn good. You just have to wait a few hours."

"You're being pretty cold to the man who just arranged for you to be pampered today."

He won't say that when he sees me in that costume. "The wait will be worth it. Promise."

"I'm holding you to that."

8

TRISTAN BROUSSARD

I sit on the bed while Emma Lia is in the bathroom changing into the red teddy I chose for her to wear tonight. I lean back, propping my weight on my arms. I probably appear carefree, but there's nothing carefree about the way I feel as I look at mon bebelle.

The drive to make her my submissive in every way is fierce. It's quickly becoming an obsession that goes beyond a simple sexual need. Though my body burns for her, I don't just want to fuck her. I want to imprint myself on her, to mark her from the inside out, so that she will never belong to any man but me.

I want to own her completely.

She opens the door an inch or two and peeks out through the crack. "Close your eyes."

"Why?"

"Because I have a surprise for you."

"I hate surprises."

"You'll love this one, so do it."

I close my eyes, and a few moments later hear the start of slow, seductive music. "Okay. You can open your eyes."

I'm more than a little surprised to see her standing in front of me, hands on hips, dressed in a black and red showgirl costume with black thigh-highs. She lifts the back of her hair from her neck and bites her lower lip as she bends at her knees, swaying her hips.

Mother. Fucker.

"It's not the red teddy you chose for me to wear tonight, but I hope you still like it."

"Fuck yeah, I love it."

She begins to move to the music, turning her back to me and slowly swinging her ass from side to side. The feathers forming the skirt oscillate back and forth, and all I can think about is what I'm going to do to that ass with the flogger.

My dick is so hard. It's as though it's been months instead of hours since I had her. It takes every ounce of my self-control to not tear off her costume, bend her over the bed, and pound into her flesh until I explode.

I control myself because I don't want this to happen too quickly. We have new things to try tonight.

"Come here," I say hoarsely, my cock straining painfully against the fly of my trousers.

She shimmies her way over and sits on my lap with her legs wide apart. She rubs her ass back and forth across my hard-on and then leans closer until her back is against my chest. She drops her head back and my mouth hovers over her ear, nipping at her earlobe. "Who do you belong to?"

"I belong to you."

"Yes. Yes, you do, bebelle." My voice is thick with lust.

I suck her earlobe and then release it as I move my hands to her proud tits standing up in her bustier. "Lie on the bed. Facedown."

"Yes, Master."

I get up and begin to undress while she slowly crawls onto the bed. "Head down, ass up."

She follows my instructions, but I see the hesitation in her movements. There is a part of her that fears me, that senses what I'm capable of. And she's right to be afraid. There is something within me that thrives on the pain of others, that wants to hurt them.

That wants to hurt her. And her vulnerability turns me on almost as much as her beauty.

Once she's in position, I'm able to see her pretty pink pussy and asshole peeking out from beneath the feathers. No fucking panties. That shit just about robs me of my last ounce of restraint.

I have to touch her.

I cup my hand between her legs, my middle finger pushing into her small opening. The warm moisture that I find there makes my cock jolt.

She wants me. She wants this. Although she isn't really sure what *this* is.

I can sense her nervous anticipation. She simultaneously desires and fears me, which is a huge turn-on. It also triggers another kind of hunger in me. A darker, more perverse desire.

Standing at the edge of the bed, I reach out and trail my fingers along her spine. She trembles under my touch, sending a sordid thrill through me, and I realize that I have everything I want and need, right here, right now.

Emma Lia. She's everything, and I couldn't ask for more.

I want to swallow her fear and pain. I want to hear her screams. I want to feel her fight against me and then melt in my arms while the sheets absorb the sweat of our sins.

She's the only woman that I've ever wanted this much. Having her here and at my mercy, ready to take her first flogging, is intoxicating. It's the most powerful drug I've ever tasted. Because the submissives who came before her were nothing more than diversions while I was waiting for Emma Lia.

I stroke the soft skin of her thighs and ass. Soon they will be striped, but for now I'm enjoying their unmarked smoothness. "Use your safe word and it ends immediately. Do you understand?"

"I understand, Master."

"Do you trust me?"

"I do, Master." She doesn't hesitate in answering. And although I'm grateful for her trust, I don't understand how she can so easily give it to me.

Bending down, I press a gentle kiss to the soft ivory skin over one of her cheeks and then caress my hand over it. "I took your submission by force, bebelle. But now I want to truly earn it."

A change comes over her body. The tension melts away and is replaced with relaxation.

I straighten and raise the flogger, bringing it down against the cheek that I just kissed. I don't use a lot of force, but she still jerks when the leather bites the skin covering the orbs of her ass. She almost instantly releases a soft whimper from her parted lips, and the sound forces the blood in my veins to rush to my cock.

She moves back into position with her head lowered, face pressed against the mattress, and arms outstretched. "Did that hurt?"

"Yes, but it felt good too."

This flogger is designed for a low-impact, stinging sensation. We'll need to build up to something with deeper impact.

I swing harder the second time and she still jolts, but to a much lesser degree. I bring the flogger down again and again, my motion taking on an entrancing rhythm. With each strike of the leather tails against her virgin skin, I slip further and further into a world where all I can see and hear and feel is her.

The reddening of her pale skin, the gasps and moans from her sweet mouth, the way her body tenses under each stroke of the flogger and then relaxes… I become lost in it.

My addiction is being fed. My needs met. My cravings satisfied. All of it is fulfilled by her—my obsession, my fixation, my addiction.

I stop when I feel satiated and admire my work. Emma Lia is now lying on her stomach, her beautiful alabaster cheeks and thighs adorned with pink stripes. So fucking beautiful.

I drop the flogger on the bed and crawl onto the bed, lying next to her. "Come here."

She rolls to face me and I wrap my arms around her, pulling her body against mine. This is what she needs right now—to feel taken care of, to re-establish our connection, to strengthen our bond. And this closeness is what I need too—to comfort her, to feel her in my arms.

I want to be her everything: her lover and her tormentor, her pleasure and her pain. I want to bond her to me physically and emotionally, to brand myself so deeply inside her mind and body and soul that she won't be able to leave me when she does finally pull that key.

I hold her close and stroke her hair slowly, giving both of us time to absorb what just happened and recover from the endorphin-crazed high that we're both riding. My soothing caress becomes more enthusiastic, my hands roaming her body with a new plan: to arouse, not just to calm.

My hand slips between her thighs, my fingers searching out that little bud at the top of her slit that I already know will be rigid and erect with longing for my touch. I find her needy clit and pet it with my index finger. My other hand grips her hair and pulls, forcing her to meet my gaze. Her eyes are dazed but filled with passion as they lock on mine.

Her sweet lips are parted when I lean down and devour her mouth with a deep, thorough kiss. She moans into my mouth and wraps her arms around my shoulders, pulling me hard against her.

My balls draw up tightly against my body, my cock aching for her slick, warm flesh. But right now, I only want to pleasure her—a reward for the way she trusted me with her body just now.

"I want to make you come."

She releases her hold on my shoulders, and I crawl down her body as she turns to lie on her back. I push her legs apart and she cries out when I drag my tongue across her bare slit. My tongue laps at her, tasting all of her sweet, sticky goodness. I tongue fuck her little cunt, the scent and taste of her making my head spin with raw lust before moving up to swirl my tongue over her clit. I'm merciless with it, flicking my tongue over it again and again.

I suck and release the needy little nub until her body begins to tense. Suddenly, she becomes rigid, every muscle in her body tensing. She shatters beneath me, her whole body trembling, and I taste that salty-sweet goodness on my tongue.

"Oh God. I'm coming. So hard."

I give Emma Lia her moment.

And then I want mine. "Turn over."

She obediently rolls to her stomach and gets on her hands and knees.

On all fours. Her ass tilted up. Her back slightly arched. Just the way I want her to be.

Damn, she's the hottest thing I've ever seen.

I can see everything. The folds of her wet pussy. Her

virginal pink puckered hole. The delicious curves of her cheeks, pink with marks from the flogger. My heart is pounding heavily in my chest, and my cock is throbbing painfully as I grasp her hips, lining up the head of my dick against her opening.

I push inside, and hot, wet flesh swallows my cock, sheathing me in her tight, slick perfection. "I don't know how you can feel virgin-tight every time, but you do."

She rocks on her hands and knees and pushes back against me, trying to take my cock deeper. And I happily oblige, withdrawing partially and then slamming back inside her. "Oh God. You feel so big inside of me."

The squeezing grip of her tight channel makes my spine prickle with pleasure. Waves of urgent need rush through me, and I lose all self-control, digging my fingers into the soft skin of her hips and thrusting with every bit of power I have inside me.

Her moans become louder, and I feel her inner muscles contracting around my cock. I try, damn, I try, but I can't stop the release of seed into her warm core.

I use my grip on her hips to hold her in place and thrust hard one final time. "I'm giving it all to you, baby."

When the last drop has left my body and entered hers, I pull out and collapse onto my side, taking her with me. Our skin is sticky with sweat, gluing us together, and we lie that way, still joined, while our breathing gradually slows.

I hold her spooned against me, and as I come down from my orgasm, I feel a sense of calm serenity wash over me. And I know that it's because of her. This woman quiets my demons. She makes me feel normal, happy even, and it fuels my intense obsession with her.

"Tell me that you liked what I did," I whisper, stroking her outer thigh. "Tell me that you liked the way I made you feel, bebelle."

She turns in my arms, rolling over until we're facing one another. She reaches out and cradles my face with her hand, her blue eyes on mine. "I love what you did to me. And I love the way it made me feel."

Relief. Pride. Satisfaction. All of it floods me at the same time.

I'm a different Dom with Emma Lia. Of course, I'm softer and gentler because this is new to her, but I want her complete trust. I want to be her addiction, same as she is mine. I want to be so invested in her that I actually became a slave to my passion and commitment and overwhelming desire to protect her at all costs.

That's when I will have become her true master.

And she'll never leave me.

9

———————————

EMMA LIA GRANT

I'm dressed and ready for dinner with no Tristan in sight. He was supposed to be here thirty minutes ago. We know what happens to me when I'm tardy but what about him?

I pick up the flogger and swat it across my hand. Maybe I should use this on him. Punish him for leaving me waiting. I wonder what he'd have to say about that.

My phone buzzes and lights up. It's *Sir*. That's what he entered as his contact name when he put his number in my phone. I didn't find it amusing in the least when he did it, but now I do. I maybe even like it.

"Hello, Sir."

"Hey, I'm sorry to keep you waiting."

Tristan Broussard is apologizing. I bet that doesn't happen often. "It's all right."

"My last meeting is running longer than expected. They want to grab something to eat and finish up. I'm afraid that you'll be on your own for dinner."

I hate eating alone. "Do you know what time you'll be back?"

"I don't. We still have to do a walk-through of the casino floor and make some important decisions."

I remind myself that this is a business trip for him. Not leisure. "Okay. Well, do what you gotta do, and don't worry about me."

"You should come downstairs and eat at the Japanese restaurant."

I hit Tristan up as soon as I saw it. I love sushi, and I was sadly disappointed to find out that he hates it. He won't even eat hibachi because he doesn't like the smell of fish that typically floats around in most Japanese restaurants.

"Omigod, yes. I would love some sushi." I haven't had any in weeks, and it's something that I usually eat at least twice a week.

I end my call with Tristan, and I'm disappointed that he didn't have something dirty to say to me. His dialogue was unusually tame for him, his words cold and stiff. He must have been within earshot of his business associates, otherwise I know that he would have said something filthy.

The sushi is delicious. Some of the best that I've ever had but I find my mind wandering, thinking about Tristan and how I wish he were here enjoying it with me. I'm lonesome without him.

No way. I did not just have that thought.

I walk out of the restaurant and scan the casino floor. The crowd. The flashing lights. The cha-ching sounds. All of it draws me in like an addict to a drug.

I want to gamble.

I need to gamble.

I have to gamble.

I choose a blackjack table occupied by men and a male dealer, one who isn't wearing a wedding band. Not that it really matters. The married ones ogle me and get distracted by my jacked-up breasts just as easily as the single ones. Maybe even more so.

I stand back and observe the game for a while before taking a seat between two older men, getting a feel for what's happening.

"Hello," the gambler on my right says.

"Hello."

"This table has a twenty-five-dollar minimum, sweetheart."

What the fuck is that supposed to mean?

I watched his game before I sat beside him, and I'm one hundred and twelve percent certain that I knew more about blackjack when I was ten years old than this old bastard does now.

I point to the brass and black sign. "Is that what the sign means? That I must bet at least twenty-five dollars on each hand?"

"That's right, honey."

"Thank you for clearing that up for me. I was really confused."

"Sure thing."

I drop a thousand bucks on the table and push it in the direction of the dealer. I never gamble at a table with a minimum of less than a hundred, but I need to keep a low profile. I know without a doubt that Tristan would be furious if I gained the wrong attention here.

According to the stats in my head, it's time for the next hand to give a probable advantage to the dealer. I have to take some losses with the wins, so I only bet twenty-five dollars. And I lose as predicted.

"Well, shoot. So much for lady luck."

"Don't fret, little lady. It's only your first hand."

I play with my chips, picking them up and then dropping them into stacks.

"First time in Vegas?"

"Is it that obvious?" Lie. I was born here. And I don't even know how many times I've been back since we moved to the Mississippi coast.

"Just a little bit."

"Are you up or down?" I giggle. "That's gambling lingo, right?"

"It is. And I'm down three thousand."

I widen my eyes. "Yikes. I can't imagine losing that kind of money."

The man winks. "Losing three thousand dollars is nothing for me, sweetheart."

He wants me to know, or think, that he has money. Might as well feed into his trap and make him feel good about himself. "What do you do for a living?"

"Manufacturing."

That could be one of a million things. "What do you manufacture?"

"Bed liners for pickup trucks."

That sounds boring as fuck. "Ooh... exciting."

"Not really but I make a lot of money doing it."

Damn, I hate when a man brags about his income. Makes me want to tell this asshole that he makes chump change compared to my boyfriend.

My boyfriend. Shit, did I really just refer to Tristan Broussard as my boyfriend? Because that's not what he is. Not even a little.

I need to think about the game. About the cards. About the bets.

Not Tristan Broussard.

I allow myself to win a few hands with some minimal bets before placing my first five-hundred-dollar bet.

"I wouldn't advise you to bet five hundred dollars on this hand."

This bastard who seems to have nominated and voted himself into the position of my gambling advisor is getting on my fucking nerves. "I think it'll be fine. I feel lucky this time."

"Wouldn't you feel more comfortable betting less? Like maybe a hundred?" he asks.

"I'm actually very comfortable with my bet." My voice drips with sugary sweetness, but I'm annoyed as hell.

"Okay. But don't say that I didn't warn you when you lose."

"I won't say a word."

When the hand is over, I drag my winning chips into my growing pile. I'm up a grand after about fifteen minutes. I could be up a lot more if I weren't playing to maintain a low profile.

"You were right, little lady."

I shrug. "I had a good feeling about that one."

I could sit here and casually win ten thousand over the next hour, but I don't think that I can put up with this man's advice in my ear.

"I feel like my luck has come to an end. I'd better cash out."

"You don't have to go so soon."

I push away from the table and stand, straightening my dress. "I should. I'd hate to lose what I just won."

He slides a stack of chips in front of me. "Put your money away and stay a while longer. You can play on my money."

This isn't a first. I've had plenty of men slide chips in front of me to keep me gambling at their table. And they all want the same thing. "And what if I lose it?"

He shrugs. "It's not a big deal. Plenty more where that came from."

Tristan is still in his meeting and probably will be for a while yet. If I don't stay on the casino floor, I'll be left to entertain myself some other way. May as well spend my time doing something that I enjoy. "All right."

IT'S ALMOST MIDNIGHT. TRISTAN'S MEETING HAS RUN much longer than expected. What kind of business meeting carries over into the night like this?

He could be with another woman. If he is, there'd be nothing that I could say about that. But if he's fucking someone else, I'd have plenty to say about that. I may owe him a debt, but he doesn't wear a condom, and he owes me monogamy until this is over. He has no right to put my safety in danger by sleeping around with other women while we're having sex.

I push all of the chips in front of me over to Craig, the man I'm on a first-name basis with now. "This has been fun, but it's time for me to call it quits."

"You can't quit yet."

"It's late and I'm really tired."

Craig leans over and places his hand over mine. "You should come up to my room," he whispers.

I ease my hand away from his. "I can't."

"I think that you can."

"I'm here with my boyfriend."

Craig smiles. "There hasn't been anyone to come by once and check on you all night long."

"His business meeting ran late, and I was on my own tonight."

"Then he is a fool for leaving you on your own tonight. I would never leave you to fend for yourself in Vegas, not even to tend to business."

Yeah, right.

I feel the touch of Tristan's hand on my upper arm before I hear his sexy Cajun accent behind me. "Bebelle."

I twist on my stool. "Tristan... what are you doing here?"

"My associates and I were walking the casino floor and I saw you. It was impossible to miss the most beautiful woman in the place." He kisses the side of my face. "But I see that you found someone to keep you company in my absence."

"This is Craig."

"I suppose I should thank you for keeping my girl occupied."

"The pleasure was all mine."

"I'm sure that it was." Tristan's eyes are narrowed, and I hear a possessive tone in his voice. "Are you ready to go up, love?"

Love?

"I am." I turn around and smile at Craig. "Good luck."

"No luck needed. I'm done too—now that my lady luck is leaving."

Tristan places his hand inside mine and leads me toward the elevators. I say lead because he's walking so fast that he's practically dragging me across the casino floor.

"Is something wrong?"

"Don't talk to me right now."

"Tristan... did I do something to upset you?"

"You heard me, bebelle." Shit. He's using his Dom tone. His command voice.

The tension in the elevator as we rise to the top floor is suffocating. I want so badly to ask him again what is wrong, but something deep inside urges me to keep my mouth shut.

He unlocks the door and holds it open for me. That's Tristan—he treats me like a queen in public and like a whore behind closed doors.

A gleam enters his eyes. It's one that could only belong to a predator, full of both heat and anticipation, making me breathless and edgy. "Are you going to tell me what I've done?"

"Bedroom. Now."

I do as he orders, turning around to face him once we're next to the bed. "Are you going to tell me?"

"You think that you can cozy up with another man while I'm your Dom?"

Is he serious? He thinks I'd bother with another man when I have him? "I didn't cozy up with that man."

"Then what did you do?"

"I was keeping myself occupied while I waited for your business meeting to be over."

"You were occupying yourself with another man."

Well, I'll be damned. Tristan Broussard is jealous. "I was gambling. He just happened to be sitting beside me."

"You belong to me, bebelle. I don't want another man to ever be under the impression that he can have you as long as you're with me."

"I told him that I was here with someone."

"And he still asked you to come to his room."

Tristan was clearly standing there listening for a while. "He asked, and I declined."

"He shouldn't have had the opportunity to ask."

"Are you going to punish me?"

"Yes, bebelle. I am definitely going to punish you."

My heart races from both excitement and fear. "What are you going to do to me?"

"I'm going to spank your ass so that you'll wear my marks

when I fuck you." The thought alone triggers a tingle between my legs. "Take off your clothes."

I turn around and lift my hair. "Unzip me?"

Tristan lowers my zipper, and my dress falls from my shoulders. I expect him to lean in and kiss my skin or whisper something filthy in my ear, but he doesn't. Instead, he walks away, and I immediately feel the loss of his warmth. I'm surprised by the disappointment that I feel.

I'm completely bare when Tristan returns, stalking toward me. "Turn around."

I turn and face the bed, awaiting his next instructions. He grabs my hands and pulls them to rest at the small of my back, binding them together with something that I can't identify. It's not cold as I would expect handcuffs to be. Maybe rope?

He pushes a finger between my wrists and whatever is tied around them. "Not too tight?"

"No."

"Put your knee on the bed." I do as he says, and he helps me climb onto the mattress.

"Like this, on my knees?"

"No. Facedown." I was afraid of that; I won't be able to see what's coming.

He helps me lower my upper body so that I don't face plant. And that's how I lie while he strips out of his clothes. I wish I could see him getting naked. Watching him is like having my own private strip show, only a thousand times better.

His hands roam my shoulders, my spine, my ass and then they move down the length of my legs, each touch sending me up in flames. He delivers a light smack over one cheek with his palm, and I immediately gasp. Then he pets the area, soothing away the hurt as the warm burn of pleasure rapidly takes over. Before I'm able to brace myself for the next one, he brings his hand down over my opposite cheek. Fire singes over my skin, but the pain disappears quickly, replaced with the warm hum of decadent, forbidden pleasure.

"How many should I give you, bebelle? How many can you take?"

I know the answer that he wants to hear. "As many as you want to give me, Master."

He rubs his palm over my cheek. "Who do you belong to?"

"I belong to you." I think he must love hearing those words from me; he asks me so often.

"I'm angry with you, bebelle. Very angry." I wait for the next swat, but it doesn't come. "I didn't like seeing you with that man, and I damn sure didn't like your gambling with his money."

"I'm sorry, Tristan. I was only passing the time while you were tied up with your meeting. I'm yours and only yours. Yours to do with as you please. You know this."

I slipped. I called him Tristan instead of Master, yet I know that I've pleased him by the warmth and gentleness of his caress as he rubs his hand over the area he just struck.

"You were made for me, bebelle." I hear satisfaction in his voice. "And yes, you do belong to me, and you are mine to do with as I please."

He pops my other cheek, causing me to flinch and then moan as euphoria swallows me. The events of the evening fade to obscurity, forgotten, as he delivers my spanking, each swat harder, stronger, than the last. He's careful to not overwhelm me. He gradually works me up from lighter to harder and as the pain increases, so does the indescribable pleasure.

"Your ass is red with my mark, my stamp of possession. So. Fucking. Beautiful." Tristan's voice is gruff as he rubs his hand over my throbbing flesh. "Tell me, bebelle. Do you want more? Or do you want me to fuck your sweet pussy that also belongs to me?"

My pussy clenches when I hear Tristan say that it belongs to him.

"I want it all, Tristan," I whisper. "I want you in me, on me, around me, all at the same time."

My words barely leave my lips before he moves to his knees behind me. He fingers me lightly, smearing the slick moisture over my lips, before spreading them apart and plunging hard and deep into my pussy.

He pumps into me over and over, his hips smacking hard against my ass. I close my eyes, squeezing hard around his cock as he rides me hard, almost brutally. I jolt when his hand swats my hip, fast and furious. The edge of pain mixed with pleasure is a heady sensation, and I close my eyes, biting my bottom lip.

I begin trembling as Tristan brings me closer to release. Just when I think that I'm going to topple over the edge, he withdraws and leaves me so very close to orgasm.

Shit. Is he going to deny my orgasm as punishment? Probably. It's much crueler than any kind of spanking he could give me.

"Please don't do the edging thing, Tristan. Please."

"I won't if you don't want me to, bebelle."

"I don't." Even as good as it is in the end, I can't take it right now. I'm too stimulated.

Fire ignites over my ass as his hand descends, taking my breath away. My chest heaves, and I inhale sharply as the pain fades, giving in to the euphoria. I close my eyes as blow after blow rains down on my cheeks, and I enter a hazy world that blurs around me where only bliss exists.

He moves behind me again and parts my folds. He enters me, forgoing his former roughness, and thrusts long and slow, setting a leisurely pace. His body lowers against mine and his hand finds the sensitive nub at the top of my slit between my legs. He leans down and presses his lips to my spine, kissing his way up to my nape. I don't feel his earlier anger anymore.

"Come, bebelle. Now."

And I do.

My orgasm floods me. It's the sweetest, slowest spasm to ever encompass my body, setting each nerve ending on fire. I tingle from head to toe, delicious chill bumps spreading over my skin, making me hypersensitive to his touch.

His hands move to my shoulders, and he uses his grasp to hold me in place when he thrusts harder. "Oh fuck. I'm coming."

I feel his cock jerk inside me, and then the warmth of his cum heats my body from the inside out.

Tristan's palm flattens between my shoulder blades and works its way down to the small of my back. My hands are suddenly freed, and he coaxes me to turn over. "Come here."

I place my hands on the bed and lift my upper body, looking at him over my shoulder. Nervous. On edge because I don't know where his head is.

Is he still angry with me for talking to that man and gambling with his money?

Tristan pulls on my arm, and this time I go to him, but I feel overwhelmed. Confused. Mostly because I crave his consolation.

He pulls me onto his lap, wrapping his arms around me. He cradles me like a child that he's comforting after a scuffed knee, and I cling to him as though he isn't the person who just spanked my ass until it feels blistered.

His hand strokes the back of my hair. "I'm very pleased with you."

I lift my face from his shoulder and our eyes connect. I

thought that he was angry with me for talking to Craig and gambling with his money. "You're pleased with me?"

"I pushed you harder this time, and you handled it beautifully. So yes, bebelle, I'm very pleased with you."

Sometimes I wonder just how far I'd allow him to go. How hard I'd allow him to push me if it meant pleasing him.

This man is changing me. But I think that I am also changing him.

And I can't wait to see who we become together.

10

TRISTAN BROUSSARD

I OPEN MY EYES AND SEE THREE GLOWING RED NUMBERS: 5:13. Not the three numbers that I need to see.

"Shit, bebelle. Get up. We overslept."

"Hmm?" she groans.

"Get up, Emma Lia. We're late." Damn. I can't believe that I fell asleep.

It was really late—or early—when Emma Lia and I stopped fucking around. I didn't set the alarm because I was going to stick it out for the hour rather than go to sleep.

So fucking stupid.

I told Emma Lia to get a little rest, and I'd wake her when it was time to get up. But she felt so good curled around me. And I was so relaxed after coming three times. I couldn't stop myself from drifting off into a bebelle-induced post-orgasmic coma.

"Can we make it?"

"It's chartered. They'll wait, but we need to get a move on so they don't cancel on us."

Emma Lia goes to her drawer of clothes and yanks out a

top and bottom. "Sorry, but it's going to be a leggings, tunic, and messy hair bun day. I won't be looking my best."

"Doesn't matter what you're wearing. You're always beautiful to me."

Emma Lia catches my attention when she pulls a pair of black lace panties up her legs. She wiggles her butt to adjust them after they're in place. So fucking sexy.

"I smell like your cum." She grins. "And like sex. Lots of it."

Sweat and cum, *my cum*, mixed with Emma Lia's feminine juices. Nothing in the world like the mix of those scents.

"I need a shower," she says.

"No time. Your pussy gets to smell freshly fucked by me until we get home." I don't hate that she'll have my mark on her all day.

A wicked grin grows on her face. "A nice reminder of last night's fuck-a-thon."

It was indeed a fuck-a-thon.

I have no idea how we pull it off, but we're walking out the door within fifteen minutes of crawling out of bed.

Emma Lia holds up her hand for a high five. "Nice teamwork, Mr. Broussard."

I like hearing her call me that. Reminds me of our Mr. and Mrs. scene when we arrived. "We make a great team."

The minute we're in the air, Emma Lia's head leaves my shoulder and we recline our seats. "See you in New Orleans."

"Sweet dreams, bebelle." Mrs. Broussard.

I sleep off and on during our flight home, but mostly off. I've never been a great sleeper during travel. Not the case for Emma Lia. She is curled into a ball and leaning against the window. Her breath is steady, and every now and then I hear a soft snore.

I'm feeling restless, so I forgo closing my eyes and crack

open Emma Lia's *The Thorn Birds* novel. Once we reach full altitude, the flight attendant makes her way back to check on us. "May I get you or your wife anything?"

Here we go again with the whole *my wife* thing, but I don't mind the charade. Especially when it involves my fucking Mrs. Broussard into oblivion. "I think that my wife is fine, but I'll take a Jack and Coke."

The flight home feels so long. Probably because Emma Lia sleeps most of the way, and I'm left to entertain myself. "I enjoy traveling, but it always feels so good to come home."

"Traveling always makes me feel icky. And it doesn't help that I didn't get a shower this morning," she says.

"I have an idea. Go upstairs and get into the tub while I get our bags out of the car. And when I'm finished, I'll join you."

She giggles. "I have a very strong feeling that if you get in the tub with me, you'll end up owing me eight keys instead of seven."

I owe her seven key pulls?

Mother. Fucker.

"Seven? Are you sure?"

"The first time was when I was Mrs. Broussard. Two was showgirl-flogger night. Three was after the spanking you gave me for talking to Craig at the blackjack table. Four was the night after we played craps until midnight. Five was after the big-stakes poker game. Six happened after you flogged me for the second time. And last night makes seven."

Damn. She's right. I've been too busy enjoying her to notice how many key pulls she's been earning. And she's not even counting the morning sex that we had. Guess she's considering those as vanilla encounters and not *charging* me for them.

Fuck, these keys are going faster than I intended. And

honestly, I thought that Emma Lia enjoyed our trip. I wouldn't have expected her to bring up the keys as soon as we walk through the door.

"Come on. Let's go pull your keys." And get that shit over with.

"It's okay. I can do it after my bath."

"I'd rather you do it now." I can't sit here worrying about this for one minute longer than necessary.

She follows me to my office, and I unlock the cabinet where I'm storing the box of keys and move it to my desk. She sighs and closes her eyes, reaching in and pulling out the first key. "One."

She repeats the process until seven brass keys are lined up along the edge of my desk. She picks up the first key and inserts it into the lock, turning it. And nothing happens.

Thank fuck.

She shakes her head. "Not this one."

She goes through the same process six more times, holding up the final key. "Last one, Broussard. Do you think this could be it?"

"I'm not finished with you and fate knows it. So, no. This key won't fit the lock either."

She pushes the key in, but nothing happens when she turns it. "You are correct. Fate seems content for me to stay with you a while longer."

Relief washes through me like a wave rushing over a beach. But then that consolation that I feel recedes when I consider that maybe next time she will pull the key that works.

"Go on and get your bath."

"Are you still getting into the bath with me?"

I shake my head. "I just gave you seven key pulls. Seven, bebelle. I'm not ready to give you another one."

"O... kay. But you know where to find me if you should change your mind."

I bring our bags up and begin unpacking while Emma Lia soaks in the tub. I go still and listen when I hear her singing at the top of her lungs. I chuckle deep down because it's so damn bad.

"Tell me you love me," she belts out.

"Are you seriously entertained by that horrid sound?"

I look up and see Claudia standing in the doorway of my bedroom. "I am, but only because it's so terrible."

"Does Miss Mundane think that she can sing?"

"She knows that she sounds horrible, yet she doesn't care." I love that about her.

Claudia walks into my bedroom toward me, but my glare stops her in her tracks. "You know that you aren't allowed in here without an invitation. And I didn't invite you."

"Do you make her stand in the doorway and wait for an invitation?" she asks.

"I did in the beginning."

"But you don't now? She gets to come into your bedroom whenever she likes?"

"Emma Lia and I have a different kind of relationship. What we have makes me feel really good inside." And I've never had that feeling before.

"You aren't a Dom with her. And she for damn sure isn't a submissive."

And here we go again. "We're everything that I need us to be and more." So much more.

She steps toward me and I hold up my hand, cueing her to stop. And she does. "I miss you, Tristan. I miss us."

"The sooner you find your new Dom, the sooner that'll come to an end. Speaking of, how is the search going?"

"I've told you that I don't want anyone else."

"Which means you haven't been looking."

"I can't."

That shit just makes my blood boil. "You must, Claudia. You don't have a choice. And I'm tiring of telling you."

"I've been thinking about it, and I see no reason that you can't have both of us."

There have been times when I would have entertained that idea. Probably even been eager for a polyamorous relationship but not since Emma Lia came into my life. "Not interested."

"It wouldn't have to be threesomes if that's not what you want. You could split your time between us."

"No, Claudia. I don't want that."

"I wouldn't tell her if you wanted to keep our being together a secret."

"I don't know how else to tell you so that you'll understand. I don't want you. I only want her." I'm so fucking tired of trying to convince Claudia of this. "Don't bring this up again. I don't want to hear it anymore."

"Tristan..."

I point at the door. "Out of my room. Now. And don't come back in here again. In fact, don't even be on this floor."

I don't want Emma Lia to see Claudia anywhere near here. Ever. Finding me with my former submissive, especially in the place where I once dominated her... fuck, I can't think of many things that would be more disastrous at this point in my Dom-sub relationship with Emma Lia. She would lose every bit of trust that I've worked so hard to build with her. And that can't happen.

EMMA LIA IS STRETCHED OUT ON HER SIDE, HER FEET

touching the side of my thigh, watching television while I go over some of the proposals for the new Vegas casino. Nothing about the way that we're touching is sexual, but I like the closeness.

"I'm tired."

"Would you like to go up and turn in early?"

"Guess that depends on what you have planned for tonight."

I hold up the stack of papers in my hand. "This is what I have planned for tonight."

"Oh." She turns onto her back and wiggles her toes against my leg. "You won't be coming to my bedroom or asking me to visit yours?"

The truth is that I'd like nothing more than for her to come to my bedroom tonight and stay until morning. I've enjoyed waking with her every day this week, but that won't happen without my owing her a key. And she's pulling too many, too fast.

"I have a lot of work to do on the new casino. I'll probably be busy for the next few hours."

"All right. I think I'll go to bed early then." She sits up and slides over to me, placing a soft kiss against my mouth. "Good night."

"Good night, bebelle."

I end up working much longer than planned. It's two in the morning by the time I crawl into my bed. I close my eyes and lie there thinking of Emma Lia in the neighboring room. At least a dozen times, I consider getting up and going to her room. And I would if it weren't for those fucking keys.

I spit in my hand and reach into my boxers, grip my hardening cock. I glide it up and down, imagining that Emma Lia is riding my cock.

Yeah, I liked it when she got on top. And I want her to do it again. Soon.

I open my eyes and see Emma Lia's shadow in the doorway between our bedrooms. Like an obedient submissive, she waits for my invitation. And I don't disappoint. "Come here, bebelle."

I throw the covers back and she climbs into bed on top of me, placing one leg over my pelvis so she's straddling me. She leans forward, her elbows pressed into the pillow on each side of my head and kisses my mouth. I place my hands on her thighs and move them upward until they reach her bare cheeks. "Bebelle, I believe you have forgotten your panties."

She kisses my mouth slowly, but something about it feels different. Less in synch. Almost clumsy. And desperate.

I pull my mouth away from hers. "I can't give you another key. Not this soon." I pause a moment. "If we do this, it has to be a freebie. Vanilla. Are you willing to do that?"

"Mmm-hmm."

"Okay. If you're giving it to me freely then you know that I'm willing."

Emma Lia moves down my body, kissing every inch until she's kneeling between my legs. She hooks her fingers into my waistband and tugs. I lift my hips and she drags my sleep pants down my legs.

She lowers her body to mine, bringing us close enough to touch, but she isn't pressing her weight against me. Her nightgown is slick when she climbs upward to straddle me again. She arches back, and my erection presses against her warm entrance.

I place my hands on her stomach and glide them up her silky gown. I palm her tits, her hands covering mine, and her nipples harden beneath my touch. She moans when I squeeze lightly, and that's when I notice that her breasts don't feel the same. They're firm, round, unmoving. And her moan doesn't sound like what I've become accustomed to hearing.

This is all wrong.

I push her off of me and lean over to twist the switch on the lamp.

Son. Of. A. Bitch.

"What the fuck are you doing?"

Claudia moves to her knees and crawls toward me. "I want you to make love to me."

"We don't make love. We never have; plus, I've told you over and over that I don't want you. Mother! Fucker! What in the hell is wrong with you that you can't hear what I'm telling you?"

She just snuck into my bedroom from Emma Lia's room and led me to believe that she was mon bebelle. This goes well beyond anything reasonable.

"I love you, Tristan. I can't let go of us."

"You don't have a fucking choice. I. Let. You. Go."

Emma Lia appears in the doorway between our bedrooms, her eyes wide when she sees Claudia in my bed. "Well, I guess this explains why you didn't want me to come to your bed tonight."

"Bebelle... this is not what it looks like."

She shakes her head. "Damn, Tristan. I wouldn't expect a Dom to be so fucking cliché."

"I'm not being fucking cliché. I'm being fucking serious."

"Do us both a favor and don't insult me. Call a spade a spade."

"I didn't invite her into my bed." I look at Claudia. "Tell her what you did."

Claudia shrugs and smiles.

"You. Fucking. Bitch."

"This woman is your long-term submissive, Tristan, and you're cueing her to cover for you."

"She's my *former* submissive," I correct. "Former, as in I no longer want her."

"She doesn't look former from where I'm standing." I see pain in mon bebelle's eyes as she looks at Claudia on my bed, wearing what I now recognize as lingerie that I chose for Emma Lia. It's the ivory piece with ruffles and a bow between the breasts. It's the sweet one I asked her to wear on vanilla night.

Emma Lia whirls around and stalks into her bedroom, slamming the door behind her.

Fuck.

Fuck.

Fuck! This is not good.

"A real submissive wouldn't dare do that to her Master."

"Can you please just shut the fuck up and get out, Claudia."

"I want—"

"I don't give a goddamn what you want." I dash across the floor and grab Claudia's upper arm, pulling her out of my bed and pushing her to the door.

"Please don't throw me out, Tristan."

"I wouldn't have to throw you out if you'd fucking listen to what I'm telling you."

I open the door and shove her into the hallway. "Find a Dom or don't. You have three days to find somewhere else to go. I'm done playing host to you."

"Tristan—"

I slam the door in her face and lock it. Dammit, Claudia may have really fucked things up between Emma Lia and me. Which is exactly what she wants.

How do I fix this with mon bebelle? How do I make her believe me when I explain what really happened?

I have no idea, but here goes.

11

EMMA LIA GRANT

WHAT A MOTHERFUCKER.

I can't believe that he had Claudia in his bedroom. And right next to my bedroom of all places. If he wanted to fuck her, he could have at least done it in her bedroom.

I want to yank every hair out of that bitch's head, but even more I want to twist Tristan's balls until they separate from his body.

Fury and resentment swirl inside me, scorching every fiber within my body, but mostly the ones in the center of my chest. Which is so fucking stupid. *I'm* so fucking stupid. I shouldn't feel anything but hatred for this man. He's my captor. My blackmailer. My Dominant. He enjoys using me and fucking me and hurting me.

He spent the last week telling me that I was his. And I spent the week warming up to the idea. I was growing fond of him. I felt a connection growing between us. I was even beginning to feel like I actually could be his. But that's what a good Dominant does, right? He convinces a submissive that she belongs to him.

I'm jealous of him being with another woman. And it's

absurd. To feel any kind of attachment to the man who is blackmailing me into sex is the stupidest thing that I've ever done in my life. But I'm also fucking pissed as hell too; he's putting my health at risk by fucking someone else.

I feel so ignorant for thinking that I was the only woman in his life. I feel foolish for caring that I'm not.

I have to get out of here.

I've made all of three steps toward the closet when Tristan comes into my room. "Bebelle…" I ignore him, and he follows me into the closet. "Bebelle…"

"I am not your doll, so don't call me that anymore." I wish he hadn't given me that endearing name. It's only made me bend more easily to his will.

"You will always be my doll."

My eyes sting and that pisses me off. I can't cry over this motherfucker. "I'm no one's toy to play with, Tristan."

"Will you please stop and listen to me?"

"No. The quicker I change clothes, the quicker I can be out of here and be on my way home."

"You aren't leaving," he says.

I whirl around to face him. "Are you going to hold me captive again?"

"I'm going to do what I must to keep you here while I explain."

"I don't want to hear your lies."

Tristan wraps his arms around my waist and hoists me over his shoulder, carrying me to the bed and tossing me in the middle. He crawls over me and restrains my wrists above my head. "You're going to listen to me whether you want to or not."

"Wanna bet, motherfucker?"

He doesn't even make an attempt to block my knee when it collides with his groin.

"Oooh... fuuuck." He instantly rolls off of me into the fetal position. "Ugggh!"

I scramble away from him on the bed. "Fuck you, Tristan Broussard. Fuck. You."

I dash into the closet and yank my gown over my head. I pull on the first shirt that I reach, followed by a pair of jeans. No bra. No time for that.

I'm pushing my foot into a sneaker when Tristan bear-hugs me from behind and carries me to the bed again, repeating the same process except this time I'm tossed onto the bed facedown. "I told you that you're going to listen to me, and you're going to."

I fight but it's no use in this position. I'm pinned against the bed. And he has me.

"You're out of your mind if you expect me to stay after this."

He grabs the back of my neck and pushes me down against the mattress so hard that I don't have a chance in hell of freeing myself of his hold. "I didn't fuck Claudia."

"You were naked, and your dick was hard. I saw it, so don't try to pull that shit on me." It kills me to have seen the proof of his desire for her, but I'm glad that I did. It's a real wake-up call.

"I was naked and hard because she came into my bedroom through the doorway between our rooms in the dark. I swear to God that I thought it was you coming to me. And that's exactly what she wanted—to make me believe that it was you in my bed. Did you see what she wearing? It was a piece of your lingerie. The one with ruffles. The one you wore on vanilla night. She knows that I'd feel that in the dark and never suspect it was her. Because she doesn't own anything sweet and innocent like it."

Shit. She was wearing my silk ruffled gown.

"The lamp was on."

"I turned it on when I realized that she wasn't you."

"How did you know that it wasn't me?"

"I felt her implants and knew they weren't your breasts."

That makes me nauseous. "Great. You were touching her breasts."

"Only because I thought she was you."

"What else did you do with her?"

"We kissed. And almost fucked. *Almost*. But we didn't."

Claudia is desperate, and she's hopelessly in love with Tristan. That much I know for certain. I can totally see her sneaking into his bed and pretending to be me if it meant she could have him again.

"I believe you."

He releases his hold on my neck and wrists. "I'm going to let you up, but you'd better not kick me in my balls again."

I turn over and sit up so that we're facing one another. "I'm sorry that I kneed you."

"Please don't ever do that again."

I don't say anything because at this point, I'm making no promises as long as that bitch is here. "Claudia has been making problems between us since I moved in, and I'm sick of it. She has to go."

The expression on Tristan's face instantly changes. "You seem to be confused about the dynamics of my place as your Dom. I'm in control, and I make the decisions. You aren't my girlfriend, and you aren't my wife. You are my submissive, and you don't ever get to make demands. I do what I want, when I want, and I don't owe you a goddamn thing. I don't take orders from you. I've known Claudia a hell of a lot longer than I've known you, and she will stay until I decide that she goes."

Wow. That stings a lot more than it should. "I think that we should end this relationship, and I should leave."

"We will if that's what you want, but understand this: if you leave, you're going to jail."

"I won't be the only one, buddy. Your crimes against me exceed my little bit of casino cheating."

"Prove it."

I glare at him, saying nothing; we both know I have no evidence of his wrongdoings.

"That's right. You can't prove anything."

He grabs my wrist when I get up, but I yank it from his grip. "Please leave my room."

I'm here because Tristan Broussard is blackmailing me. Somewhere along the way I seem to have forgotten what he is and what he's doing to me. But no more. He just gave me the perfect reminder of what kind of bastard he really is. And I won't be forgetting anytime soon.

I don't want to be here, and I don't want to do this anymore. That key is my ticket to freedom. I have to pull it soon, get the fuck out of here, and never see Tristan Broussard again.

And forget that all of this ever happened.

It's been three days since my fight with Tristan. I've avoided him; I'm so pissed off and hurt that I don't even want to look at him. And apparently, he must feel the same since he hasn't come to me. But not seeing him—and not fucking him—isn't at all beneficial for me. Staying away from him may satisfy my need to lick my wounds in private, but it doesn't bring me any closer to gaining my freedom.

I don't want to be the one to give in and seek him out, but I want the hell out of here more than I want my pride to remain intact. Sulking around in my bedroom isn't doing anything but extending my stay.

There's a knock at my bedroom door, and I already know that it's Ray bringing in my dinner tray. "Good evening, miss."

"Hey, Ray."

He slightly lifts the tray. "Same place?"

"The bed is fine."

He places the tray on the foot of my bed and lifts the cover. "Crawfish-stuffed catfish with a Cajun cream sauce. I must warn you: it'll clear your sinuses."

"I'm not worried. Everything you cook is delicious."

"Thank you, miss. It's nice to prepare meals for someone who is appreciative of my culinary skills."

"Tristan is highly appreciative of your cooking." I can't believe that Ray would think otherwise.

"I'm referring to Claudia."

"She doesn't like your cooking?"

"She's very critical and often offers advice on how I can improve."

Why does that not surprise me?

"Well, that's ridiculous. You are magnificent and need no one's advice. Don't listen to that cunt." I look up at Ray. "I'm sorry. I shouldn't have said something so vulgar to you."

"She is a cunt, and I look forward to her departure. A year is a long time to put up with her."

I can't stop myself from laughing at Ray. "Well, you shouldn't be expecting her departure anytime soon. Tristan plans on letting her stay as long as she likes. He was quite clear about it."

"I thought that Mr. Broussard would be eager for her to leave now that you're here."

I smile, shaking my head. "I'm afraid not."

"Well, that's extremely disappointing."

"It is indeed."

"Mr. Broussard has been... we'll call it *easily irritated* since you stopped joining him for dinner."

"Good." I'm glad that his balls are chafed, but he shouldn't be salty to Ray because of it. "I'm sorry. I don't mean that I'm happy he's being short-tempered with you."

"I understand your meaning."

"Is Mr. Broussard taking dinner in the dining room tonight?"

"No, miss. He asked me to hold his dinner while he finalizes some business in his office."

In his office—right next to the keys. Perfect. I can slip in, do what I gotta do, pull my key, and get the hell out.

"Is there anything else that I can get for you?" Ray asks.

"Can't think of a thing."

"All right, miss. Enjoy."

My dignity and appetite vanish and are replaced by nausea as I mentally prepare myself for what I must do if I'm to be free of Tristan Broussard's hold over me.

I don't knock. I don't speak. I simply enter Tristan's office, shutting the door behind me, and make my way around his desk to where he's sitting in his chair. His eyes widen and one brow lifts. He leans back in his chair and the corners of his mouth tug upward, but only slightly.

I lower myself to the floor, kneeling before him, and position myself between his thick, muscular thighs. Normally I would glide my palms up his legs, teasing him and giving him time to become fully erect. But not this time. I want this to be over and done so I can pull my key.

I tug at the button on his trousers and then lower the zipper. Untucking his button-down, I shove it upward to his waist. His hardening cock jumps out of his boxer briefs when I pull down the elastic waistband.

I keep my head down, never making eye contact with him. That's what he likes in his submissive, but I choose to keep my eyes lowered because I can't bear to see an ounce of satisfaction on his face.

I tilt my head to the side, forming a curtain with my hair over one shoulder. I want him to watch. He loves the sight of his cock in my mouth, and it'll get him off faster.

I hold the base and forgo the licking and teasing that I would normally do. I simply open and take him into my mouth. Breath hisses between his gritted teeth, and he pushes his fingers into my hair, cradling the back of my head. His head drops back to rest against his chair and he lifts his hips a little to thrust into my mouth. "Take it in all the way."

I breathe deeply and mentally turn off my gag reflex when I lower my mouth down the length of his shaft until the tip hits the back of my throat. The taste of salty pre-cum fills my mouth. "Oh, that's it, bebelle. Just like that."

Bebelle. Hearing him call me doll makes me want to stop and slap the shit out of him. I am not his bebelle. If he really thinks of me as his doll, he wouldn't have spoken to me the way he did. And he wouldn't have chosen her over me.

I hate doing this for him. I hate bringing him pleasure when he has treated me as though I don't matter. And if it's an empty body without feelings that he wants, then that's what the fuck he's going to get.

I close my eyes and turn off every feeling and emotion inside me. The anger, the sadness, the disappointment—I bury all of it so deep that it'll never see the light of day again. I become a robot, using my body only as a vessel for earning my next key.

"Fuck, you're good at sucking me off."

Good. Maybe that means he's about to come and this can be over.

I flatten my tongue and move with him, taking his cock over and over, the swollen head hitting the back of my throat. I take a quick breath and wrap my hand around his base, stroking and squeezing his length every time he slides in and out of my mouth. Saliva drips down his length and on top of my hand, making it slide up and down his cock with ease.

He plunges into my mouth faster, thrusting so hard that I make that terrible gagging sound that he loves so much. His gentle hold on the back of my head transitions into his hand fisting my hair.

My jaws, my neck, my knees—all of them are aching. I'm ready for this to be over so I tighten my hand around his dick and suck harder.

"Fuck, I'm going to come."

He pushes himself deep, and I feel the warm jets of cum hitting the back of my throat. "Swallow all of it."

He pulls out of my mouth following the last spasm and reaches for my hands, pulling me to stand. His eyes connect with mine, and I see the happiness that was there prior to three days ago. But it doesn't make me forget the things that he said to me.

"I've missed you, bebelle."

He cradles the sides of my face and leans in to kiss my mouth, but I pull away. "I'd like to pull my key."

His subtle smile vanishes. "That's what this was about?"

"You were very clear about what I am to you and what I am not. What else could this have possibly been about?"

He drops his hands from my face as though I've burned him. "I thought that you'd come to make up."

No. He thought that I'd come to grovel.

"This was about earning a key. Nothing more, nothing less."

"All right." He steps away and moves toward the cabinet. "You earned it."

Same as last time, he removes the box and places it on his desk. I finger several keys and silently pray for my fingers to find the key that will unlock that padlock.

I remove one from the box and hold it out in the palm of my hand. "This one."

He hesitates, looking at the key in my hand for a moment before taking it. "Feeling lucky?"

"I'll tell you after you try the key in the lock."

He pushes it in and turns. And nothing happens.

"No. I don't feel lucky at all."

I turn without another word and leave his office, running the statistics in my head as I walk to my bedroom. Twelve percent of the keys are gone. My odds are slowly swinging more in my favor. Every key pulled puts me one step closer to freedom. I just have to hang in there a little longer.

12

TRISTAN BROUSSARD

I wanted to go to Emma Lia's room last night. I wanted to make things okay with her. But I couldn't do it. I'm a Dom. I can't bend for her. Not again. I've already bent more than I ever should have. She is my submissive, and she needs to understand what that means.

It's been twenty-four hours since she came into my office and sucked me off. And fuck, I can't believe how badly I want to see her again. I'm sitting in my office pretending to work because I'm hoping that she'll pay me another visit tonight.

I sit patiently, and she doesn't disappoint.

Same as last night, she enters my office without knocking and closes the door. Not saying a word, she rounds my desk and bends over it. Her hands grasp the back of her dress and she pulls it upward, exposing her naked ass and pussy.

Feels like every drop of blood in my veins rushes to my cock, making me hard in record time. But truth be told, I was already semi-hard thinking—and hoping—she'd come to me again.

"Look at me."

She shakes her head and says nothing.

"It doesn't have to be this way, bebelle."

Her head lowers, and her palms flatten on the top of my desk. "This is the position that you like best."

"You know that's not what I mean."

She still doesn't look at me. "I'm here to be your submissive, fulfill my part of our agreement, and earn my key. That's all."

I hate the defeat and emptiness that I hear in her voice. I'd prefer that she fight instead of seeming as though she couldn't care less.

I place my hand on the back of her thigh and caress it up her leg. "I don't want it to be like this, bebelle."

Her dress slides down and partially covers her ass. "Are you going to fuck me or not, Tristan?"

My words have hurt her. And I hate that. I didn't mean to cause her pain, but she must learn that she is only my submissive. She doesn't have a say in how I run my life.

I get up and move behind her, undoing my pants. "Yes, bebelle. I'm going to fuck you."

I wish that I were stronger. I wish that I could tell her I won't take her this way, but the truth is that I can't resist. I'm obsessed with her, and I'll take her this way if it's the only way that she's willing to give herself to me.

I touch her pussy and find that she's dry, but not for long. I'm going to make her want this even if she doesn't want to want it.

I dip my fingers into my mouth and then use my wet fingers to lubricate the skin around her entrance. I guide my cock inside her and her body accepts mine, not easily at first, but the following thrusts gradually come with more ease.

I reach around her waist and spread the top of her slit. Although I'm certain that it's unintentional, she softly moans when my fingertips expose her hooded clit. I rejoice inside;

she may be pissed off at me, but she can't turn off those pleasure receptors or her response. She can't hide her arousal from me. And I'm going to use that weakness to bring her back to me. Back to the place that I had worked so hard to get to with her.

I watch my cock move in and out of her from behind, slow and deliberate. I could fuck her hard only for my pleasure, but I want to make her feel good too.

She softly moans again as I flick her clit with my fingertips and rocks against me, pushing and pulling herself on and off of my length faster.

"Slow down, bebelle. Don't rush it." I need to make this last as long as possible. I'm not sure when she'll let me fuck her again.

I lower my face to her shoulder and lean around to kiss the side of her neck and face. She might not have allowed me to kiss her mouth last night, but she can't stop me from kissing her this way.

Her pussy contracts around my cock, and I grip her tightly as the pleasure rocks through my body. I enjoy the high, and I ride it to the very end, feeling my body tense and relax as the pleasure enters and leaves my extremities. I thrust those final times, filling her with my seed until all of it is inside her instead of me. Right where it should be.

I rest my forehead against her upper shoulders, my cock still inside her, and wrap both arms around her. I love everything about the way she feels in my arms.

"You owe me a key, Tristan."

My cock has gone soft and slips out of her when she squirms beneath me.

"And what will you do if you pull the correct one this time?"

"I'll be out of here so fast that your head will spin."

I thought she would say that but hearing her say it still stings.

I straighten and fasten my pants before unlocking the cabinet and follow the same procedure as the previous times. She drops her hand inside and digs around in the box with her eyes closed. Probably praying. And her face is the epitome of stoic when she hands over the key.

I insert it and turn. Again, nothing happens. Thank fuck.

My racing heart begins to calm a little. "Not the one."

She says nothing before turning and leaving my office. And while watching her walk away, I can't remember a time when I've ever felt emptier inside.

What is this woman doing to me?

Emma Lia is my submissive. She is my joy. And now she is also my pain.

I WAITED IN MY OFFICE FOR TWO HOURS BEFORE DINNER, and Emma Lia didn't come to me. I'm not sure what that means. I'm only certain about one thing: knowing that she is in my house within my grasp but is staying away is killing me.

Like every other night since our argument, I lie in my bed hoping that mon bebelle will open the door that separates our rooms. She wouldn't even need to ask permission to enter. I would welcome her with open arms.

I hear the sound of soft music, a severely melancholy tune, coming from her room and it's minus her usual singing. I'd give anything to hear her terrible singing right now.

I open my laptop and attempt to occupy my mind with the Vegas project. Burying myself in work—instead of Emma Lia—is what I've done to take my mind off of our falling-out.

I look over when the door between our bedrooms opens

and... holy fuck. Emma Lia is standing in the doorway wearing a garter belt with fishnet stockings and a red and black corset-style top that pushes her tits up and out. Of course, I chose it, but it's a sexier piece of lingerie than she normally wears. And fuck. I lower my face and look over the top of my glasses, seeing that she isn't wearing the panties that go with it. Her pussy is completely bare.

"I'm inviting you to join me in my room tonight."

That's all she says before going back into her room, leaving the door open.

Well, fuck. Looks like she's turning the tables on me tonight. And of course, her MO works. She knows that there's not a chance in hell that I would turn down this opportunity.

She's standing beside the kinky cabinet with the doors open. "What would you like tonight, Master?"

Never in a million years would I have imagined walking into her bedroom and hearing that question tonight. Not after the last four days. And I don't know how to answer because I want it all.

I reach inside to the top shelf and take out a harmless toy. "I would like you to wear this collar and leash."

She comes to me and turns, lifting her hair, allowing me to place the black leather collar with O ring around her neck and secure the buckle. She turns around and my cock twitches when I see her wearing it. And I can't resist wrapping the leash around my hand and pulling her in to kiss her mouth.

There's no passion in her kiss. It's like pressing my lips to an empty body.

"What else would you like?"

I remove my next choice from the cabinet. "The nipple clamps."

She unlaces the top of her corset and her tits fall out of the top. "Would you like to apply them, Master?"

Fuck yes. "I would very much love to apply them."

I adjust them so the pressure will be minimal. We'll need to build up to more pressure.

She winces when I close the first clamp and tighten it. "Too much?"

She shakes her head. "It hurts, but I can take it."

The sadist inside me loves hearing her say that it hurts, but it's not enough for him. I tighten the clamp until she cries out. "Ohhh... Tris... tan."

I could correct her, remind her that she's to call me Master in the bedroom, but I actually like hearing her say my name right now.

I apply the other clamp around her hard bud, and she closes her eyes, sucking air in through the tight O that her lips form. The sight of her delicate nipples clamped and hurting turns me on in a way that most people would find disturbing.

"Ohh... fuck, Tristan. That hurts."

Her face is tense, and I know that she's telling the truth, that her sensitive nipples are likely in agony from the vicious bite of the toy. Just the way that I want them.

Cupping the undersides of her breasts with my hands, I squeeze them lightly, molding the soft flesh with my fingers. "Hurts, doesn't it?"

"Yes, Master."

She jerks when the movement of my hands pulls on the chain between her nipples. "Sure you can take the pain, my sweet bebelle?"

She nods slowly. "What else do you want from me tonight?" Her words come out in a ragged whisper.

Damn. I like this one-eighty in Emma Lia.

I remove a paddle because I want to punish the fuck out of her for avoiding me these last four days. "This. Because I'm dying to spank your ass for what you've done to me this week."

There's a small tug at each corner of her mouth. "Why did you not choose the butt plug?"

I wasn't aware that it was a choice. "The butt plug?"

She reaches into the cabinet and takes out the blue jewel. "Why did you not choose this?"

"Because you told me no anal. You were very adamant about it, and I don't feel like now is the right time to push it after the week that we've had."

"How badly do you want to fuck my virgin asshole?"

She knows how much I want it. I've been telling her for weeks. "Right now, I can think of nothing that I want more."

"What would you say if I told you that I was willing to give it to you?"

Is she serious? Because this isn't something that you joke about. "I would ask what you're up to."

"I want my debt to be paid off as soon as possible. And I want to use my anal virginity as a bargaining chip."

She has my attention. "I'm listening."

"Your cock gets to fuck my virgin asshole... in exchange for twenty keys."

"*Twenty*?" A two with a zero behind it? Did I hear her correctly?

"No fucking way. That's twenty percent of the keys gone in one night. Actually more than that since you're down to eighty-seven. It's too many. I can't risk it."

She places the plug back in the cabinet. "What if I had nothing to prepare me? You get straight-up, non-stretched anal. One hundred percent tight virginal bum fun."

Fuck. It's like I'm an addict and she's offering me one of the best hits of my life. How does one resist when he has zero willpower to say no?

I'm shaking because I want this so badly. "You know that I want it. Badly. But we have to negotiate that number."

"Make me an offer."

"Five."

She laughs. "We both know that it's worth far more than that."

She isn't wrong, but I can't give in and offer more than the minimum she's willing to take. "What kind of number do you have in your head?"

"I've already told you. I want twenty keys."

"That's too high, bebelle. You have to negotiate with me."

"Actually, I don't have to negotiate with you at all."

"I want it, but I won't give you twenty." I could lose her tonight if I agree to twenty. The odds are just too much in her favor. As much as I want my cock inside that tight hole, I can't take that kind of risk.

She comes to me and takes my hand, turning it over and placing the leash inside my palm. "You want it, but I also know that you don't just simply want it so you can get off. You want to fuck it hard and see me cry because you're stretching me so wide."

The Dom inside of me wraps the leash around my hand, and uses it to pull her close to me, face-to-face with my mouth touching hers. "When I take your ass for the first time, you will cry, bebelle. Real tears. Because I won't take it gently. I won't care that it's your first time."

"Do it, Tristan," she whispers. "Fuck me until I cry."

Fuck! Does this woman realize that she's toying with one of my deepest, darkest desires where she's concerned?

Of course, she does. That's why she's doing this—offering me what I want most in the world so she can pull those twenty keys.

And leave me.

My cock is throbbing behind my boxer briefs and sleep pants, and I have this intense desperation inside that begs me to say to hell with the consequences. Tears and a tight hole, two of my favorite things. I should take what she's offering. The proposition might not come around again.

But twenty out of the remaining eighty-seven keys? That's almost a twenty-three percent chance of pulling the right one. She has an almost one-in-four chance of clearing her debt and leaving me tonight.

How lucky do I feel?

I'm a gambling man, and I fucking love winning when the odds are stacked against me.

"I'm going to tear your ass up, and then after you pull those twenty keys and none of them work, I'm going to tear it up again while you're bent over my desk, crying and begging for mercy."

Her lips curl around her teeth as she tries to contain her happiness. She really thinks that she has just earned her freedom. "You're only partially right, Tristan. You may tear up my ass once, but then that padlock is going to pop open, and I'm going to walk out of this house. I'm never going to see you again after tonight."

Those words feel like a harsh slap across my face.

"We'll see, bebelle."

I glide my hand down her satin-and-lace corset and cup my hand over the soft exposed lips between her legs. I push a finger through the center and this time find that her pussy is soaking wet, causing my cock to throb for her. My little submissive is aroused, and the struggle to keep my hunger for her under control is nearly too much to take.

I touch her engorged clit, and she bites her bottom lip as she softly moans and adjusts her hips forward, a silent plea for me to give her more. "You like that, don't you?"

The tip of her tongue comes out, flicking between her naturally peachy-pink lips. "I do."

I cease the movement of my fingers and she whimpers, clear indication that my torture is having an effect on her. "Oh please."

"Please what?" I prod, coaxing her to plead.

"Please don't stop."

Emma Lia hasn't been treating me as her Dom lately, but she's going to now. "Beg me for it, bebelle. And tell me what you don't want me to stop."

"Please touch me." She tilts her hips upward, causing my fingertips to drag over her clit. But we're not playing that game. I want to play something entirely different. Every sensation that she feels, I want it to be so intense that it makes her forget the pain she feels when I push my cock into her ass.

I move my hand, depriving her of my touch altogether. "What is it that you want me to touch?"

Her throat bobs when she swallows. "My clit."

"You know that those two barely whispered words aren't going to cut it with your Dom."

She clears her throat. "Please rub my clit, Master," she says louder.

"Tell me again and this time say my name."

"Please rub my clit, Tristan. Please."

"All right, baby." I touch her again, pushing my fingers into her slick folds to stimulate that sensitive bundle of nerves with light, even strokes. "Like that?"

"Yesss, just like that." Her breathing becomes faster. "God, Tristan. No one makes me feel like you do. No... one."

I use the leash to pull her closer. "You can't come, bebelle."

"Please don't say that. I'm almost there."

"I said that you can't come, and I meant it." I take my hand away. "I want you on the bed."

She walks to the bed and crawls onto it on her all fours. "No. On your back."

I walk toward her while she moves into position. A sharp gasp escapes her mouth when I grab her ankles and yank her across the bed until her ass is on the edge. After placing her feet on the bedrails, I push her knees apart. Lifting her head from the bed, she looks at me kneeling between her legs. "You've deprived my mouth of your pussy for days. I'm in withdrawal, and I need a taste before I can go any further."

Her head falls back against the mattress when I flatten my tongue and lick her in one long upward sweep. Her pussy is drenched, but I allow saliva to drip out of my mouth so it can run down her crack and be used as extra lubrication when I move on to her other hole.

She lifts her hips from the bed in a rhythmic, rocking motion and pushes her fingers into my hair, tugging hard when I insert my fingers and pump them in and out while I suck her clit.

"Ohhh, Tristan. I can't believe how much I've missed your mouth on me."

I've learned Emma Lia's body and how it reacts to my touch. She'll come very soon if I continue. And I have other plans for that orgasm.

I stop licking her pussy and move my fingers from my non-dominant hand through the slick moisture before moving them to that puckered hole. I rub it slowly in a circular motion, and her body instantly tenses, the hole clenching tightly. "Relax, bebelle. I'm only touching you right now."

She breathes in through her nose and blows the breath out through pursed lips.

"I'm going to push one finger inside now. It'll feel strange and new, but it won't hurt if you relax."

"All right."

She clenches her muscle around my finger. Instinct, I'm sure. "Relax, baby. Let the muscle go lax."

The tight squeeze around my finger releases, and I advance it farther. "That's my good girl. Keep relaxing."

I thrust the one finger in and out slowly, and her body gradually begins to rock with the motion of my hand. And I bet that she doesn't even realize it. "You're doing so good, baby. I'm going to give you two now."

A second finger enters and it's the same reaction. Tense. Relax. Except this time, she does it without being prompted.

I repeat the same procedure, thrusting in and out slowly. "Does that feel good?"

"Yes," she whispers, as though she might be ashamed for liking something so dirty and taboo.

"I knew that you'd like it."

As much as I want to continue playing with her, I can no longer wait to fuck that ass.

I remove my fingers and adjust her placement on the edge of the bed; she did quite a bit of squirming while I was eating her pussy.

I reach for the bottle of lube I got out of the kinky cabinet and push her legs back. She begins to tremble when she registers what's coming next, and it's in this moment that I really realize how scared she is. And her fear turns me on even more.

I slap her ass and dig my fingers into her flesh. "Fuck, I've wanted my cock inside your ass since that very first time that I saw you in my casino. I've waited for months, and now it's finally going to happen."

I squirt the lubrication directly on the small puckered

opening between her ass cheeks, right below her already glistening pussy.

She whimpers when I position the tip of my cock at the entrance of her tight little asshole. "Oh God. This is going to hurt."

Her fear and hesitation please me in the most twisted way, but it also shows me how much work I have ahead of me in molding her into my perfect submissive.

I rub the head of my cock through the lube on her ass, coating it in the slickness for an easier entrance. I'd love to shove my cock into her right now and hear her sharp intake of air, but I don't want to make this a bad experience for her. I need her to want to do this again.

I position the head of my cock at her entrance for penetration. "Relax."

"I'm trying, Tristan."

I push lightly, and her body accepts the first inch of my cock, but then I hit a wall. A sharp exhale leaves her mouth. "Ohhh... fuck. That already hurts."

"Bear down a little."

"What?"

"Bear down like you're trying to push me out."

"I'm not doing that."

"Trust me. It'll make it feel better."

Emma Lia takes several deep breaths, and then I feel her sphincter open when she follows my instructions. I waste no time rocking in and out, advancing my cock gradually until I'm sheathed entirely, ignoring her attempts to squirm away.

Her ass is so tight around my cock that I'm shaking from the effort it's taking to control myself. "You feel so fucking good." My voice is gruff and thick with lust.

"It's burning... oh God... I can't... Tristan, please... you're stretching me too much."

"Stay with me, bebelle. I promise that I'm going to make you feel good, but it's going to take a little work."

I go still, my cock all the way in her ass. My hand pets her pussy, spreading her juices all over her soft folds. My fingers lightly rub her clit in a circular motion, and it isn't long before she's breathing deeply and rocking her hips against my hand.

I pull my cock back slowly and advance again, a shiver running down my spine because the pleasure is so intense, and this time she doesn't protest. Explosive pleasure shoots through my balls as her ass squeezes my dick. I withdraw from her halfway and plunge back in, savoring the feel of her body's compression around me.

She cries out when I drive into her, the sound a mix of sobs and gasping as I fall into a rough, rhythmic pace. And that's when I look at her and see the tears. The real kind. The kind that I love. But I'm torn inside. I have an intense desire to hurt her and protect her at the same time.

"Do you want me to stop?"

She breathes in deeply. "No. Maybe you could just go slower?"

Leaning forward, I press a soft kiss to her lips. I then brace myself over her with one hand and we're face-to-face with barely any space between us. "All right, baby."

I slowly knead the top of her wet slit and thrust into her with care. Her moans take on a different sound—pleasure and ecstasy instead of pain.

My orgasm approaches with sudden intensity, my spine tingling as my balls constrict. I stave off the orgasm for as long as I can, hoping that she'll catch up with me, and then her ass contracts around my cock. Her muscles spasm rhythmically around my cock, and she cries out beneath me. And I realize that she's coming.

"Oh God, Tristan... I'm coming."

I hear her tell me that she's coming, and it triggers my orgasm like a bomb. It's a jolt of intense pleasure surging through my body as jets of cum spurt into her deepest, darkest depths, leaving me astonished and breathless from the power behind my release.

I carefully pull out of her, and she lies there limp and boneless. I release both nipple clamps and she doesn't react—until blood rushes back to the assaulted buds. A moan leaves her mouth, and tears well up in her eyes as her hands go to her breasts, holding pressure over them. Small sobs shake the delicate frame of her body.

I was too aggressive. I should have gone easier on her; she wasn't ready to go that far.

I move to sit on the bed and pull my girl onto my lap. My arms wrap around her body, and I rock back and forth gently and sweetly as though she's a child that I'm trying to console. And I'm thrilled when she buries her face against my shoulder and sobs. Why? Because I know that it means she craves consolation from the one who hurt her. More proof that she is accepting her place as my submissive.

"We're not done, and fate knows it. You won't pull that key tonight."

"I know."

My dark soul rejoices, drinking in her acceptance of our relationship. Her submission may not be given in the traditional manner, but it is mine. And I hope that it's enough if I'm the one who loses when she pulls those keys tonight.

13

EMMA LIA GRANT

Twenty keys—and not a one of them opens that heart-shaped padlock. Tristan wins again. Luck remains on his side, and that thrills the fuck out of him.

He grins and drops the final key into a box with the others that didn't open the padlock. "Will you stay with me tonight?"

I'm still angry with Tristan for allowing Claudia to stay in his house. "No."

His brow lifts. "No?"

"I don't want her here after the shit that she pulled, and things will not be okay between us again until you send her away."

"Things will be okay between us again if she leaves?"

"Yes."

"Okay."

"Okay what?"

"Consider her gone."

I almost melt when I hear those words. He's bending for me, and I think that it's only fair for me to do the same. "I'll stay with you tonight."

"Would you like to take a bath together?"

I took a bath an hour ago, but I just had my ass reamed. Things feel a little out of sorts, and I think that immersing in water would feel good. "I would love to soak the bum."

"Are you in pain?"

"Not pain. It just feels... not the same."

"I loved fucking you in the ass. It was singlehandedly the most amazing fuck that I've ever had. Nothing has ever topped that experience."

I was a little afraid that he had built it up in his mind to be this fantastic experience and that it would fall flat for one reason or another. But he says that I'm the best fuck that he's ever had. That's saying a lot, considering how much sex he's had.

"I can't say that I loved anal. It hurt at first. A lot. But it did feel good toward the end."

"It was good enough that you came."

"I certainly did." Like a stick of dynamite.

"I don't want tonight to be the last time that we do that."

I smile. "We'll see."

"You're using my own words on me, bebelle. I like it."

Tristan and I soak in his claw-foot tub until our skin prunes and the stinging hot water turns lukewarm. He helps me out of the tub and then wraps me in a fluffy white towel like I'm a child. And it's not the first time that he's treated me like a child tonight.

He pulled me onto his lap and rocked me when I was hurting. His caress didn't comfort the pain in my nipples or the tenderness in my ass, but it did soothe me emotionally. And I liked it very much.

I think about the dynamics of our relationship as I brush my teeth. He hurts me because he needs that for his satisfaction, and then he soothes me afterward, which is what I need for my satisfaction. I'm beginning to understand how a Dom-sub relationship can be truly satisfying—as long as a still-interested ex-submissive isn't in the picture. I'll never be okay with that.

We finish brushing our teeth, and Tristan moves behind me. He kisses my bare shoulder while I watch him in the bathroom mirror. He looks up and our eyes meet as he pushes my hair away from the side of my neck, leaving a trail of kisses to that sweet spot below my ear.

And fuck me, I melt against him.

He sucks my earlobe into his mouth and glides his hand around my waist until it's cupping me between my legs. His fingers toy with the nub at the top of my slit, and I'm astonished by how well he knows my body and what it needs to reach the ultimate pleasure.

With his free hand, he reaches for my chin, grasping it and forcing me to watch our reflections in the mirror. "Look at me. I want to see your face when you come."

I grasp his wrist and open my mouth, sucking two of his fingers into my mouth. I suck hard and my subdued moan vibrates around his fingers. Feeling the soft flesh of his skin and tissue but firmness of his bones between my teeth, I have a sudden desire to bite down. And I do. He hisses and then I soothe my bite with a suck and lick.

My skin tingles as I imagine his mouth licking me. His hands worshipping me. His cock stretching me.

I need him.

Now.

"I want to feel you inside of me."

He presses a kiss to the side of my face. "I'm sorry, but I just gave you twenty keys. I can't afford another tonight."

"No key." He's sending Claudia away, and that has made me very happy. I'm feeling generous. And horny.

He smiles, and I see how happy he is with my offer. "Are you sure?"

"Yes, but we do it my way." I twist in his arms and drape my hands over his shoulders. "I want it slow and sweet, on the bed, and face-to-face."

He nods slowly and placing his hands on my hips, uses them to guide me, kissing en route on the way to the bed. "I can do that."

I know he can do it. He's already demonstrated that he can do it very well, but I want him to want to do it.

And I shouldn't. Desiring such things could destroy me. I know this, and yet it doesn't change the way I feel.

Tristan stops midway and cups my ass, lifting me so I'm straddling him with my legs around his waist. He carries me to the bed and lowers our bodies together, his body lying on top of me. I love the feel of his weight pressing me into the bed.

His hand glides up the side of my body and cups my breast from the underside, his thumb lightly circling my nipple. "I won't ever ask you to wear the nipple clamps again."

"I would try them again but maybe just not so tight next time."

His lips claim the side of my neck while his hand navigates its way down my body. It dips between my legs, rubbing up and down, petting me. I part my legs wide, giving him full access to my body, and my shallow breath moves in and out of my chest quickly as I anticipate his next move.

He pushes a finger through my slick center and back up once in a slow, torturous stroke that barely grazes my clit. I'm desperate for more, so I impatiently move against his fingers.

He chuckles. "You need more, huh?"

"A lot more."

He rubs his fingers up and down, every upward stroke applying direct pressure to my clit. "Feel good?"

"Mmm-hmm."

He changes his technique and rubs me in a circular motion. My back arches off the bed, and my legs fall even farther apart. A soft whine slips from my mouth when Tristan stops and moves to kneel between my legs. But I know what's coming and I'm elated.

He presses his lips to my inner thigh and trails kisses up my trembling legs. It's impossible to stop squirming beneath him. He moves upward and nibbles the skin of my groin, making me involuntarily convulse, before he grabs my thighs and pushes them back and apart.

He places his tongue against my center and drags it in an upward sweep. Slow. Soft. So good I want to scream.

"Want things nice and slow like this?"

"Mmm-hmm. I like that a lot."

The movement of his tongue continues—light, gentle, careful. All of the nerves around my clit and vagina are highly responsive to the new sensations. It's only taking a small amount of pressure and movement to stimulate me toward orgasm.

"Feels so good, Tristan."

The sensation in my pelvis climbs and then tops out, causing my legs to tense and toes to curl. Tingly warmth floods my face, neck, hands, and feet as I ride my orgasm to its fullest extent.

I allow my legs to slide down the mattress until they're outstretched when my orgasm ends. "That was so good."

Tristan licks my blissful pussy one last time and then crawls up my body. He lies on top of me once we're face-to-face, the brunt of his weight supported by his arms pressed into the mattress on each side of my head. His breath is a mixture of mint and me.

I put my fingers in the back of his hair and toy with the short bristles along his neckline as he settles between my legs and reaches for his cock. But I want to slow this down. "Kiss me the way you would if you loved me. Like you would if I really were Mrs. Broussard and you adored me."

I want to see what a Dom considers love, even if it is pretend.

He stills for a moment, his eyes locked on mine, and I expect him to refuse at any moment. But he doesn't. Instead, he kisses me with so much passion that I feel as though I could black out.

When he stops kissing me, I bend my knees and let them fall apart to accommodate his body. He guides his erection to my entrance and pushes into me gently until he's fully sheathed. He closes his eyes and lightly groans. "I don't care how we do it. Fast. Slow. Hard. Soft. You always feel like pure heaven."

His pace is unhurried. He pulls back with leisure and gently advances into me again. I rock my hips away when he pulls back and tilt them upward when he thrusts. The movement comes naturally without any thought at all.

"I'm going to come."

I wrap my legs around him and dig my heels into the cheeks of his ass, pressing my pelvis and groin to his. "I want it deep inside me."

He's motionless with his cock inside me as deep as possible. And that's how he stays for the next several minutes—inside me, unmoving except for more passionate kisses like the ones that made me nearly black out.

His forehead presses to mine when he stops kissing me,

and we stay that way with him on top of me. With him inside me.

"You know how you need domination? Well, I need connection and affection. Even if it's not real, I need to feel it."

He kisses my mouth and pulls out of me slowly. "If there's anything that I understand, it's need. And I want you to have what you need."

He lies beside me and pulls me closer so I can place my head on his chest. His arm wraps around me and I toss my leg over his. I imagine we must resemble a pair of vines intertwining with each other.

I feel his heart pounding hard against my face, but it can't be from strenuous activity. He didn't fuck me fast and furious. This Dom's heart is racing for another reason.

"I want you to move into my bedroom."

I lift my face from his chest and our eyes lock. "Are you sure you want that?" He has never allowed a submissive to stay in his room.

"I'm sure that I want to fall asleep with you beside me every night, and I want to wake and see your face every morning."

"Okay."

14

TRISTAN BROUSSARD

WE'RE TWO MONTHS INTO THIS DEAL. THE INEVITABLE IS going to happen any day now. She gets closer to pulling that key every time we fuck. I know this, and yet I can't stop having her. I try. God knows that I try, but it's useless.

I don't even know how many times that I've squeaked by without her pulling a key. Vanilla nights. That's what we call our tame encounters. I treat her like my queen, but then there are times when I need to be a hard-core Dom. Can't lie. I fuck her in the ass and treat her like a whore. And she lets me... because she likes it.

My little submissive is gradually becoming everything that I had hoped for. And I don't know what I'll do when she pulls that damn key.

I could go into the box and take it out. That ensures that she'll be here a while longer, but it's only temporary. And I risk her being furious if she figures out what I've done.

I could come up with another blackmail scheme. Or just stick to the one I have and go back on my word to clear her debt. And again, risk her being furious with me.

Or I could let her go because I care more about her happiness than my own.

I'm a selfish bastard, and I won't apologize for that. I also won't apologize for the intense desire I have to keep Emma Lia in my life. She's literally the best thing in it. Ever.

And I can't let her go.

"You are cruel, Tristan Broussard." Her words are little more than a pant and whisper as she tugs on the ropes securing her to the bed frame.

I admit that I get off on tormenting her this way—bringing to the edge of orgasm and then taking it away. Because I know how explosive her orgasm will be in the end when I give in and allow her to finally come.

"Your orgasm is coming, but you must be patient and let it come when I decide you're ready."

"But I'm not patient. I want to come now," she groans.

"I know, bebelle. And you will...when I decide the time is right. Because...?"

"Because I am yours to do with as you please."

"That's right, my good girl. Now tell me again that you're mine."

"I'm yours, Tristan."

I spank the fleshy part of her hips, really only a light tap as a reminder. "Master."

She smiles, and I know that her saying my name instead of Master wasn't a slip. My girl likes the sting of my palm smacking her flesh.

"I'm yours, Master."

This has been the best month of my life. Claudia's moving out was a game changer for my relationship with mon bebelle. Had I known that my former submissive's departure would bring on this kind of change in Emma Lia, I would have insisted that Claudia go to Easton's the day that Emma Lia moved in.

I lie on my side, stretched out next to Emma Lia, and pet her crotch. "Tell me, bebelle. How does your pussy feel?"

"Thoroughly teased and tormented and tortured."

She has no idea how much that pleases me. I part her lips, find her clit, and pinch it between my thumb and index finger.

"Oh God. It's too much... too sensitive."

I'm sure it is. I used a clitoris pump on her earlier, and the little nub is swollen from the rough treatment it has undergone.

"Okay, sweet bebelle."

I watch her face as I insert two fingers into her vagina and massage that walnut-feeling nodule of sexual nerves in the roof of her pussy. "Better?"

"Omigod, yesss."

I advance my fingers deeper, my fingertips grazing the string of her IUD, and I'm reminded of what Cat told me about leaving it alone and everything would be fine. But if I pull the string, the birth control device could come out. And Emma Lia could become pregnant.

A pregnancy.

A baby. *Our* baby.

I'd have her. And when she pulls the working key, it won't matter. She wouldn't leave me if we were having a baby.

She. Wouldn't. Leave. Me.

But she would be furious when she figured out that I was responsible. She might hate me for making that kind of choice without her. *If* she found out.

The consequences of my decision would be a life-altering change for both of us. Would I consider doing something so extreme? Create an innocent life to be used as a pawn for holding onto the woman that I'm obsessed with? I realize how demented it is, even for a ruthless bastard like me.

But I always get what I want. And I'm not ruling anything out at this point.

15

EMMA LIA GRANT

THREE DAYS WITHOUT TRISTAN. FUCK, I DIDN'T THINK IT was possible to miss him so much in such a short amount of time.

A problem popped up with the Vegas project, and he wanted me to go. Ordered me. Commanded me. He may have even resorted to a small amount of begging and pleading, but I couldn't skip out on my nana. Not when it's her seventy-fifth birthday.

I've enjoyed spending time with my family and friends these last few days. Being back in Biloxi has been fun, but I miss Tristan. I miss New Orleans. And he misses me based on his last text.

TRISTAN: I should be home by 7:00. I want you in our bedroom on your knees, ready to suck my cock when I walk through the door. And I want it deep.

EMMA LIA: Do you want me naked or wearing lingerie?

TRISTAN: Naked. I don't have the patience for undressing you tonight.

EMMA LIA: I will be ready for you, Master. Naked and kneeling, my mouth eager for your cock.

TRISTAN: That's my good girl.

Oh, Tristan. There isn't another man in the world like him.

Most women would be insulted or offended by his harsh words, but his orders only manage to make me wet with anticipation. But there are two words in his text that stand out to me like none other.

Our bedroom.

There is no longer Tristan's bedroom with his submissive's bedroom next door. We share one room. One bed. One bathroom. We have breakfast together in the mornings, and then he goes to work, leaving me at home like a trophy wife. He comes home in the evenings, and we share dinner before going to bed and fucking like savages. Unless it's a vanilla night. He's been offering those to me more and more lately. At first, I thought it was so he could get laid without giving me a key pull, but I'm beginning to think that he enjoys vanilla more than I do.

We live like a married couple, except kinkier. And I like it. I'm content with being Tristan's submissive... who he often fucks in the ass.

Seven o'clock approaches, and I take my place on the floor

beside our bed. I know that I might have to stay this way for a while, but Tristan will reward me when he sees the reddened impressions on my knees and lower legs.

I've only been on my knees for a few minutes when there's a knock on the bedroom door. "Miss..."

It's Ray's voice at the door. "Just a minute," I call out.

I panic mildly as I quickly pull on a pair of yoga pants and oversized T-shirt. Ray never comes to our bedroom for any reason.

I answer the door and Ray's face is apologetic. "I'm sorry to bother you when Mr. Broussard is on his way home, but his father has just arrived. I thought that you might want to receive him since you're the lady of the house."

The lady of the house? I guess that must be a nice way of calling me the woman who is currently fucking the gentleman of the house.

"Yes. I should receive him, but not like this. Would you tell him that I'll be out in a moment?"

"Certainly, miss."

I change quickly into a casual dress and ballerina flats, leaving my hair and makeup as it is. Thank goodness I was ready for Tristan's arrival so that much is done.

I'm suddenly nervous as I descend the stairs to meet the man that my father wanted me to avoid. And I still don't know why. Perhaps meeting Mr. Broussard will shed some light on that.

Ray is standing at the bottom of the stairs when I reach the first floor. "He's waiting in the library."

"Thank you."

Tristan's father is standing with his back to me, holding the photo of Tristan with his mother, but he spins around rapidly when he hears the creak of the wood plank flooring beneath my feet.

Despite the thirty-something-year age gap, I'm immediately taken aback by Tristan's resemblance to him. By blood, this man is the brother of Tristan's mother. I wouldn't have expected him to share so many similarities. It's like seeing a preview of what Tristan will look like in his sixties.

"Miss Grant?"

He knows my name? "Yes, I'm Emma Lia. It's lovely to meet you, Mr. Broussard."

"Emma Lia. A beautiful name for a beautiful girl."

Oh, I can see right now that this one is charming. "Thank you, Mr. Broussard. Tristan tells me the same thing."

He returns the photograph to its place on the table. "How old are you, dear?"

Well, he doesn't waste any time getting down to it. "Twenty-two."

"Mmm... so young. Much younger than my son."

"Fourteen years. It felt like a much larger age gap before I came to know Tristan, but now it feels like nothing." I don't even think about it anymore.

"How well do you know my son? Or rather how well does he know you?"

"We've only known one another for a few months, but we spend a lot of time together. We've come to know one another quite well."

He stares at me, making me feel a bit self-conscious. "I'm not sure what it is, but something about you reminds me of my sweet Lisette."

I don't recall Tristan mentioning anyone by that name. "Lisette?"

"She was Tristan's mother."

"Oh." Lisette Broussard. What a pretty name. But the way Joseph Broussard said it led me to believe that he was speaking about a beloved rather than his deceased sister.

"Tell me, Miss Grant. Does my son know you well enough to see you for the greedy little cunt that you are?"

Whoa, wait. "Excuse me?"

"You're a greedy little cunt who is after my son's money. At least admit it."

This is completely out of left field. "I'm not after anything from Tristan."

"Every money-hungry bitch that I've ever met has said that."

I can't believe the one-eighty in this man. "I have plenty of my own money. I don't need Tristan's."

"And where did your money come from, Miss Grant?"

His tone leads me to believe that he knows quite a bit about me. "That's my business."

"I know who you are. I know your good-for-nothing father, and I know your whore grandmother. All of you are nothing but a bunch of cheats and thieves."

We are cheats in the casinos. I can't deny that, but I'm not going to stand here and be insulted. "Tristan will be home soon. You may wait here if you'd like to see him, but you and I are done talking."

I turn to leave, and I'm only about three steps toward the library doorway when I'm grabbed from behind and pushed face-first against the wall, pinned from behind. "No one walks away from me."

I buck wildly to loosen his hold on me, but he's surprisingly stout for a man of his age. "What do you think you are doing? Take your hands off of me."

"Listen to me, whore. You are going to leave this house and never see my son again."

"Take your hands off of me." I twist and use my hip to try to knock him off balance, but instead, his grip on the back of my neck tightens until the pain is excruciating. "Stop. You're hurting me."

He chuckles against my ear. "I would expect one of my son's women to have a higher tolerance for pain."

He knows what Tristan is?

He grasps my arm and twists to the point that it feels like the bone might snap at any second. "Listen to me carefully, Miss Grant. Your relationship with my son ends now. You'll never see him again."

Because my arm is in so much pain, I can hardly hear what he's saying. I have to make the pain end, and I do so by slamming my head backward, making contact with the center of his face.

"You fucking bitch."

The collision of my skull with his is hard. Maybe a little too hard since I'm seeing stars. But the stars don't stop me from seeing the drops of blood collecting on the wood flooring. I'm not sure if the blood is his or mine. Probably mine since I suddenly feel lightheaded.

"Raaay…" I try to call out for help, but my voice is muffled when Joseph Broussard's hand comes around to cover my mouth.

He drags me from the hallway back into the library, and I lose one of my ballet slippers on the rug as I struggle against him.

"Get the fuck off of her," Tristan roars as his father's body is yanked off of me. Pure physical exhaustion takes over the muscles in my body, and I crumple boneless to the floor. And that's where I'm lying when Tristan punches his father, sending him also to the floor. "Never touch her."

Joseph Broussard is lying on the floor only a few feet away, glaring at me. "She's Conrad Grant's daughter. A cheat. A thief."

"Get the fuck out of my house. Now, before I kill you for putting your hands on her."

"Son..."

Ray rushes into the library. "Sir..."

"Ray, would you please escort my father to the door?"

Tristan's arms are around me instantly, lifting me from the floor and cradling me like a baby as he carries me up the staircase. He kicks the door shut behind us when he enters the bedroom and gently lowers me to the bed. But I don't release my hold around his neck. If anything, I squeeze tighter. "Don't let go of me, Tristan."

I need to feel Tristan's soothing touch, his gentle, yet firm hold. My Dom's protective embrace is what I yearn for.

He stretches out on the bed and lies beside me, pulling my body close to his. "I'm so sorry I wasn't here. I didn't know he was coming, and even if I had, there's no way I could have predicted that out of him. I've never known him to do anything like that."

"I don't understand what happened. I didn't say or do anything to provoke him. I only answered his questions. I swear."

"Your father warned you to stay away from us but wouldn't tell you why. I've never had any kind of problems with Conrad, so I can't be the reason that he hates the Broussards. It must go back to something that happened between your father and mine. I'm convinced of that after seeing that explosive episode out of my father."

I didn't care why my father hated the Broussards, but Joseph Broussard's attack changes everything. "I have to know what provoked your father to lash out at me that way. And I'm going to find out from my dad."

"I'm going with you; I need to know what happened too."

～

My father opens the front door and pulls me into his arms, squeezing me as though we've not seen each other in forever although I just spent the last three days with him and the family. "Are you all right?"

"I'm fine."

He releases me and looks me over from head to toe. "Did that bastard hurt you?"

How does he know that anything happened to me?

I look at Tristan for an explanation. "I called Conrad while you were changing clothes."

Tristan didn't tell me that he had spoken with Dad.

I smile, not mentioning that my neck, head, and arm are throbbing and aching. "I'm a tough cookie. You know that."

"I know, but you're still my little girl, and I don't like hearing that you've been hurt in any kind of way."

"I'm okay, Dad. Really. Tristan stopped him before he was able to do much to me." Lie. That man was able to do plenty that hurt before Tristan came in and stopped him.

"Thank you for protecting my little girl."

"It's my place to protect her, and I hate that I wasn't there to keep him from laying a single finger on her."

A part of me blossoms every time I hear him profess his role as my protector.

My father looks at Tristan, his eyes slightly narrowing. I'm certain that he's dissecting his words and what they mean. I pray that he doesn't suspect the origin. I would die if he ever found out that I was Tristan's submissive. And then Tristan would die. Because Dad would kill him.

Dad, Nana, Tristan, and I move into the living room. I sit close to Tristan on the sofa, his hand possessively resting on my thigh. Our nearness and physical contact doesn't escape my dad and Nana's attention. I see it in the way they're studying us.

"Do you and Tristan's father have some kind of bad history?"

My dad breathes in deeply and sighs. "Not exactly. My history is with his younger sister, Lisette."

"You knew my mother?" Tristan asks.

"Yes. I knew Lisette well. She was my girlfriend. My first love."

Dad's girlfriend? His first love?

I recall what Tristan said about his biological father—that his mother never named his father—and I immediately have a sickening feeling in my gut.

Please don't. Please don't say those words. Please don't say that you are Tristan's father. He can't be my brother. Not after the things that we've done together.

Tristan's hand grips my leg, and I know that he must be thinking the same thing.

"Mom was a blackjack dealer at Broussard's Vegas casino. That's where I met Lisette."

I look at Tristan, but his eyes stare straight ahead. He won't even look at me.

"I was practicing my card-counting skills at a blackjack table one night, and Lisette sat beside me. She threw some hundreds on the table and joined the game. I had no idea who she was or that she was only sixteen."

Shit.

Shit.

Shit.

"Damn, she was gorgeous. That olive-tone skin and those pale blue eyes. She was the most beautiful girl I'd ever seen."

The Broussards. They are beautiful people.

"A month went by before she told me who she was. But it

didn't matter by then. I didn't care that she was the younger sister of the casino owner or that she was only sixteen. I was completely smitten with her. But Joseph cared. In fact, he cared a lot. The man cared far more than he should have."

Tristan fidgets next to me, unable to sit still.

"Joseph was sixteen years older than Lisette and had been raising her for a couple of years following the death of their parents. At first, I thought Joseph was simply an overprotective brother, but as time passed, I began to see a very unnatural relationship between them. Joseph didn't act like her older brother or even a father figure as one would expect. He behaved like a jealous lover."

Tristan's grip tightens on my thigh and when I look at him, I see that the carotid in the side of his neck is pumping like crazy.

"Lisette didn't tell anyone that she was pregnant with you. She was sixteen and scared to death... so she did what a child does. She lived in denial for months, pretending that the pregnancy wasn't real, but there came a day when she was too far along to deny it anymore. Everyone thought I was the father, but that wasn't possible. I never touched her that way. But I know who did."

I place my hand on top of Tristan's, wrapping it around his tightly. He's gone thirty-six years without knowing who his father was. And now he's finally going to know.

My dad moves to the edge of his chair and turns so he's directly facing Tristan. "There is no easy way to say this to you." My dad looks at Nana and then back at Tristan. "Joseph Broussard was sexually abusing your mother. And he is your biological father."

"No," Tristan says beneath his breath.

"She confided in me when she could no longer hide the pregnancy. I told Mom and we reported the abuse, but Joseph had more than enough money to make his problems go away. He fired Mom from her job as a dealer and had some of his thugs beat me to within an inch of my life. They beat me to the point where I almost died. I imagine that this episode with him tonight stems from my knowing his dirty little secret. He wanted Emma Lia out of your life because he's afraid of exactly what's happening right now—his exposure. I don't enjoy causing you pain, but nothing gives me more pleasure than exposing that sick bastard for what he did to Lisette."

"He told me she died in a drunk-driving accident."

"There was no car accident. She overdosed on sleeping pills."

Tristan is silent and unmoving for a moment before he pulls his hand away from mine and stands. "I need a minute to myself if you'll excuse me."

My heart hurts for Tristan. It truly aches in a way that I've never experienced for another person until this moment. I can't imagine how Tristan must be feeling right now.

"I know you don't like Tristan, but still, that must have been a gut-wrenching thing to tell him."

"Tristan is part of Lisette, and I cared for her dearly. For that reason, it's not possible for me to hate him, but he does have his father in him. And that part inside him scares me for you."

"Tristan is very good to me, Dad. He treats me like a queen."

"He'd better," my dad says. "I wouldn't tolerate you being mistreated by him. And I'll kill Joseph if he puts his hands on you again."

"I don't think that'll be necessary. Not after seeing the way Tristan went after Joseph." He chose to protect me without hearing anything that his father had to say.

I get up from the sofa, anxious to check on Tristan. "I

need to make sure he's all right. And if I had to guess, we won't be coming back inside."

"Understandable."

I say my goodbyes and go out to find Tristan sitting in one of the chairs on the front porch. I don't say a single word—not I'm sorry, not are you all right, not can I do anything to make you feel better? I don't say a word because I know how to bring comfort to my Dom.

I lower myself to my knees and assume the submissive pose at his feet. With my head bowed, I press the side of my face to his inner thigh and wrap my hand lovingly around his leg.

His hand gently grasps the back of my neck, kneading the tense muscles there. "You know exactly what I need."

The Dom inside of Tristan feels as though he has lost control. The need to regain that lost control is clawing its way through him from the inside out. "I am yours to command, to do with as you wish."

"We'll stay at the suite tonight. I don't have it in me to drive home." Tristan leans forward and lifts my face, kissing my mouth hard. "You should probably expect to use the safe word tonight."

"I'll resist."

"Use it if you must. It exists because I don't want to hurt you."

I don't want to hurt you. Those words are laughable.

"Yes, you do. You want to hurt me. You need to hurt me."

He cradles the sides of my face and presses his forehead to mine. "I wish I didn't need it, bebelle. But fuck, I do."

I place my hands on top of his. "I need what you need. Whatever it may be."

"You really mean that, don't you?"

I nod. "I do."

I have given him every part of myself. And he has taken it all, shaping me into the submissive I am meant to be.

I kneel only for him... and I am adored.

I am his whore... and I am his queen.

I am a submissive... and I belong to him.

I am his.

16

TRISTAN BROUSSARD

I'm the product of a thirty-two-year-old man raping his sixteen-year-old sister. That thought doesn't leave my mind on the drive to the hotel.

Maybe that's why I'm the way I am.

Emma Lia and I enter the front door of my hotel suite, and she doesn't take two steps before I grab her, pushing her back firmly against the door.

I take her mouth in a hard, brutal kiss, using my grip on her jaw to hold her in place. My lips smash against hers, my teeth nipping her lower lip, and then I roughly push my tongue into her mouth. It's only the first way I plan to invade her body tonight. The first way that I plan to hurt her.

She groans and the sadistic savage living within me delights in her response to the pain. But he wants more. And he gets it when I taste the metallic coppery flavor of her blood in my mouth.

"What is the safe word, bebelle?"

"Rouge," she whispers into my mouth.

"Say it when you reach your limit. And trust me, you will

reach your limit tonight." Her body tenses against mine. "Are you afraid?"

She nods. "Yes."

Her fear wakes the darkest, most predatory piece of me—the broken fragment inside that has the desire to conquer and devour her. The fury and hurt and shame I feel about my creation burns white-hot, fueling the fire of my demented craving.

"But I'm also excited and eager to see how far I'm able to go for you," she adds.

"Me too."

"I want to make you happy."

"And you do, bebelle. Every day." Releasing her jaw, I take a step back. "Bedroom. Now."

"Yes, Master."

"Take off your clothes and lie on your back in the center of the bed."

"Yes, Master."

I go to the wet bar while Emma Lia prepares for me, and I pour a whiskey, my intention being to drink enough to take off the edge. But one drink doesn't do the trick, so I pour another. And then another. I down six generously filled glasses, and with my senses and disturbing desires dulled, I feel that I am able to go to Emma Lia.

She's just as I commanded—naked and lying in the center of the bed. I never wondered if she'd be any other way. Mon bebelle obeys my directions flawlessly. Her obedience heightens my lust, my desperate hunger to possess her.

I take off my jacket and toss it over the chair in the corner, going to work on my tie next. "Bend your knees and spread your legs. I want to look at your pretty little pussy."

I toss my tie to the chair and work on the buttons of my

shirt. "Touch yourself. Rub your clit with your fingers... in a circular motion the way you like it."

She watches me undress, her eyes on mine, while her fingers circle her clit.

I break eye contact with her and go to the drawer where we keep our sex toys and apparatuses. I choose the nipple clamps, rope, and spreader bar. I have something special in mind. Something very special indeed.

I climb onto the bed and bind her wrists to the bed frame. "Not too tight?"

"No."

She studies the movement of my hands as I fasten one of the black leather cuffs of the spreader bar around her ankle. "I've been wondering when we were going to use this."

"Just been waiting until the time was right." I close the buckle of the second cuff and grip the bar in the center, pushing her legs toward her head and bending her body in half. "And the time is right."

I lower her legs to the bed and move up her body, dragging my lips over her soft, smooth skin until I reach her chest. I pull on one of her nipples and roll it between my thumb and index finger. I want to suck it into my mouth, but I don't. The slick moisture of my saliva will cause the clamps to slide.

I close the first clamp and relish the sound of her hissing in pain. "Too tight?"

Her body stiffens. "For you, I can take it."

I press a kiss to the top of her breast above her nipple. "And knowing that makes me so fucking hard for you."

I stretch beside her on the bed after the second clamp is in place, and I simply take in the beauty of what she has allowed me to do to her. Holding her chin with my hand, I place a kiss to the side of her mouth. "You are always beautiful, but even more so when you are bound."

"No ropes or handcuffs or bars are needed for me to be bound to you." Her voice is as soft as a whisper.

"And that's how I want to keep it." And I have the plan for how I'm going to make it happen. The idea has been in my head for a while, but my decision wasn't solidified until tonight.

I push myself up, rising onto my knees. She stares up at me, her lips swollen from the harsh kiss we shared when we entered the suite. "One more thing."

I go to the drawer of toys and return with a blindfold, slipping it over her eyes, before turning on "The Sound of Silence," a dark and heavy rendition of the song by Disturbed. Perfect song for my currently dark and heavy mood.

I crawl onto the bed again and kneel between her legs. And because I can't resist tasting her, and because I can't resist giving her pleasure to go with the pain, I lift the bar and go down on her.

Her body jolts when my tongue touches her, and I'm certain that she gasped. I love that sound, and it always make my dick harder, but I couldn't hear it over the music.

I flick my tongue over her clit and glide my fingers into her pussy. I pump them several times, coating them in her juices, before plunging them in all of the way.

My hands are large and my fingers long. It isn't difficult to find the string of her IUD at the mouth of her womb, especially since I've located it multiple times already and know exactly what it is I'm feeling for.

This woman has been in my life for three months, and they've been the best three months of my life. I've never known a happiness like this before. Ever. I don't want to go back to the emptiness I felt before her.

And tonight... fuck. Hearing that shit about my mom and her brother... my dad... there's no way that I could handle tonight without her. I don't know what I'd be doing right now if she weren't here for me.

She makes everything in my life better, and I've made up my mind. I won't let her go.

I love her.

I clutch the string between my index and middle fingers and pull. The fucker is slick, and it doesn't feel like it gives at all before I lose my grip on it. But I'm persistent and make another attempt, this time holding a tighter grip. And it gives. I pull gently and slowly until I'm holding a little T-shaped birth control device in my palm.

I drop it in the covers and reach out to release her ankles from the bar. The nipple clamps come off next and then the binding around her wrists. I lower my body to hers and push the blindfold away from her eyes. And I see the confusion there.

I cup my hand around the side of her face. "I was wrong about what I need tonight."

"Whatever it is, I'll give it to you."

"I want to connect with you. Bind you to me. Not bring you pain."

"Yes." Her hands come up to cradle my face. "I want that too, Tristan."

I look at Emma Lia and recall the times when she's been at her most beautiful: the night I saw her in my casino for the first time; the first time she came; when she showed me how good vanilla could be; when she played the part of Mrs. Broussard. I thought she was beautiful all of those times, but I see her in a different light tonight. She's going to be the mother of my child. And the way she looks beneath me right now... it isn't something I know how to label. Beautiful doesn't begin to cover it. I'm in awe.

I love you, Emma Lia Grant. Fuck, I wish I could say

those words, but my tongue isn't capable of forming them. Not yet, but I'm going to tell her. Soon.

"Kiss me." She grasps the back of my neck and pulls me down so our mouths can meet. I open, and our mouths make love. Slow. Deep. Loving. It's the perfect kiss for what's about to happen.

I'm overcome by what I feel for this woman and by what could happen tonight. She could possibly take a part of me into her body and join it with hers to make a baby. Half her, half me.

I understand that it can sometimes take time. I just hope like hell that I have enough time to make it happen before she pulls that key.

She stares at my eyes as I hover above and runs her fingertips down my cheek. "Tonight feels different."

"Because it is different."

Her legs are parted, and I nestle my body between them until my hard cock is against her warm, inviting entrance, ready to enter. She lifts her hips and my tip glides inside her, but I take over from there, pressing my hand into the mattress and wrapping it around her lower back. I lift to pull her hips upward and sink into her as deep as her body will allow.

I'm moving inside her slowly, and my hands move to skim the underside of her arms. I push them over her head and lace my fingers through hers. Our hands are joined as one, just like our bodies.

"I love being inside of you."

"I love it too."

I release her hands and move mine down her body, grasping her bent legs on each side of my hips and pushing them back. She moans when I slide my hand between our bodies to that place where we become one. No beginning. No end.

I've come to know mon bebelle's body as well as my own. She needs something more and I find that spot—the one that drives her crazy every time I touch it—and stroke my fingers over her clit. A moment later, her breath quickens as she grasps my back and pulls me against her tighter, grinding her hips upward. "Right there, Tristan."

Her legs tighten, and I know what will come next. And then it happens. Her inner walls squeeze around my cock, contracting in rhythm. Once. Twice. And then again and again until I lose count because I'm lost in my own world coming apart. Exploding inside her. Filling her womb with my seed. Hoping that one tiny part of me will join with that very special part of her.

I push her legs back and apart, thrusting as deeply as possible one last time. I'm making this one count. But it wouldn't be a shame if she doesn't get pregnant tonight and we have to do this over and over again.

I can't believe the extreme measures I took to prevent a baby, and now I'm trying to put one inside her. A baby. The thing I once thought I'd never want has now become my greatest desire. What a difference three months and falling in love can make.

My upper body is braced on my elbows as I hover above her. With my cock still inside her, unmoving, I push the hair away from her face. I press my forehead to hers. "You are mine."

"I am yours." Emma Lia's hands grasp the sides of my face. "And you are mine."

And you are mine. My head jolts upward when I hear her say those words; many times, she has told me that she was mine, but never that I was hers. And there is a difference.

A submissive belongs to a Dom. A Dom never belongs to a submissive.

But I belong to her.

To be continued in
Their Destiny: Book 3

ALSO BY REBEL ROSE

Lock and Key Series
Her Debt: Book 1
His Deal: Book 2
Their Destiny: Book 3

ABOUT THE AUTHOR

Rebel Rose is a decadently dark romance author living in the beautiful city of New Orleans. She prefers anti-heroes over Prince Charmings and often uses her own sexual experiences in her novels. She can typically be found somewhere in the French Quarter enjoying a cup of coffee while people watching.

Keep up to date with Rebel Rose by following her on social media at:

facebook.com/RebelRoseAuthor

instagram.com/authorrebelrose

bookbub.com/authors/rebel-rose

Made in the USA
San Bernardino, CA
27 January 2020

63690977R00109